STORIES FROM BETWEEN TWO WORLDS

Carmen Baldera

MADE FROM THE HEART

DEDICATION

I dedicate this book to all those who, like me, have experienced extraordinary events, such as impossible visual phenomena, extrasensory occurrences, intense paranormal encounters, dreams that feel like the reality itself and nightmare-like realities, moments of delight with the light, and battles with the darkness. To those who have faced sleep paralysis, extraterrestrial abductions, glimpses of the future, time travel, instant telepathy, spontaneous materializations, astral journeys, and visits from unknown beings.

TABLE OF CONTENTS

ACKNOWLEDGMENTS

This section is reserved to the people who have supported me along this narrow path, which is the truth and the life. First and foremost, I want to mention my brother, Andrés Alberto García Baldera, followed by my sister, Rosaura García Baldera (Sari), who encouraged me from childhood to write a book recounting my personal experiences. I extend my gratitude to Leonarda Baldera for her unwavering support in this work.

I also want to mention Genara Valentín (Nara), my great and dear friend, who insisted that I must compile my stories and put them on paper to share them with the world. Special thanks to my son, Alexander Mora García, who had always wished for me to create this book.

Finally, I must mention the young Jhamil Andrés Coronel Tamay, who has been a tremendous help in completing this work through the editing and transcription of the audio recordings where I narrated my lived experiences, preserving their original and authentic essence.

INTRODUCTION

In the stories contained within this book, I will unveil through my experiences, the worlds of the mystical, the strange, the ancient, the magical, the religious, the spiritual, the shamanic, the solitary, and the paranormal. These terms aim to describe phenomena that, within the current level of consciousness of some individuals, remain unknown because they did not have the opportunity to experience anything beyond the five senses.

These dimensions are not perceptible to our physical eyes, as they lack the capacity to perceive other spectrums of electromagnetic waves. The vibrational frequency at which the atoms of our eyes operate possesses just the right density to work on Earth. However, there is another kind of eye that allows us to see and sense these other dimensions, often called the third eye or the eye of God. This book is not written to convince anyone to believe in the existence of these worlds but to share the experiences of Carmen Baldera, whose life has been a carousel of contact and direct interaction with these alternative realities.

These are stories that might lead anyone to think madness is a daily occurrence, but that is far from the truth. We hope this book clears up some doubts and answers the questions of those who have longed to know more about topics that venture beyond the conventional into the controversial.

THE CURSED HOUSE

A move awaited me, and I had to prepare my items for the new adventures and daring challenges that I had to face at work. My new home was located in the north of Puerto Plata, Dominican Republic, a completely new environment, tailored to the activities I would carry out within the company on which I was a new member at the age of just eighteen.

The majestic decor, rich in artistic detail, adorned every corner, wall, and ceiling of this disproportionately large and luxurious house, creating an air of mystery. This atmosphere was particularly intensified by an object that stood in the middle of the living room. This item seemed to belong to the house's former owners, as it showed clear signs of wear and age. It radiated an aura of bygone times, a relic from an era when others had walked the same floor as me.

After organizing the chaotic assortment of boxes, clothes, and daily belongings, I was utterly exhausted. All I could think about was taking a shower, eating, and resting to regain my strength. After a long four-and-a-half-hour journey, I felt disoriented and slightly dizzy. Once I finished preparing my clothes for the next day, I noticed the kitchen clock striking ten at night.

The darkness of the night was falling over the city and over me, so I decided to retire to my quarters.

My grandmother used to say that after this hour, the dark shadows and abhorrent beings from the afterlife begin to roam the streets, parks and cementeries; so I choosed going to sleep as soon as possible. Considering the hour and already dressed in my pajamas, there was nothing else I needed to do, so all that was left was to lie down and try to fall asleep and rest. Rest peacefully? Hm! I wish. My comfort was terrifyingly interrupted by a loud yet familiar sound coming from one of the rooms on the first floor.

Although the atmosphere was far from ideal for walking through the darkness toward that creaking noise, which seemed to have a life of its own, I was not afraid of it. Curiosity drove me to get up and investigate, determined to solve the auditory mystery. After crossing the chilly hallways of the first floor, the strange sound grew louder, and the air began to fill with a deeply ominous energy. The increasing volume made it easier to pinpoint the exact location of the noise. I found that the rocking chair was moving on its own in a ghostly and deranged manner, as if the gestures rocking it were the work of some maniac who had completely lost its own mind.

The sight terrified me enough to return to my room as quickly as possible and go back to bed. Though for the rest of the night, the lights in the house would remain on as my only company against the mystery. Over time, I managed to calm my fears and doubts, making the idea of resting once again within reach. I remember very clearly that approximately five to ten minutes had passed when my ears began to pick up new sounds that, though easily recognizable to me, should not have been possible in a house where I was the only inhabitant.

What or who could possibly be moving the pots in the kitchen at such late hours of the night? To make matters worse, as I kept paying closer attention, I began to hear a distinct yet ghostly human voice that, based on my approximations, belonged to an older adult male.

Fueled by a courage and bravery that only God knows where it came from, I rushed downstairs, ready to confront whatever extraordinary being might be causing such a racket with the kitchenware.

I would have much preferred to see something tangible there, for the horror I encountered that night was far more than unsettling. When my gaze settled on the kitchen, there was nothing, no one to whom I could attribute the origin of that voice or the sounds of pots being moved roughly. A deadly silence filled the house, further unsettling my already fragile ability to connect with the lands of the dreams.

Anecdotally, I find it noteworthy that these anomalies occurred intermittently throughout the house, intensifying the ambience of mystery that enveloped it. There were weeks when events occurred every three to four days, while on others, the phenomena would persist relentlessly. The television would sometimes turn on by itself, whispers could be heard in the rooms and hallways of both the first and second floors, and occasionally, the lights would flicker on and off without anyone touching the switches. A similar phenomenon occurred with the water faucets in the bathrooms and the kitchen. Thanks to my intuition and perception, I came to realize that all these disturbances were the work of the spirit of someone who had once lived within these same walls.

Based on this premise, I decided to make a courtesy call to my brother Alex and invite him to stay temporarily in the house with me, hoping to share new memories and experiences as siblings who deeply care for each other.

After some little bit of talk, he agreed to visit me, unaware that we would soon witness some of the most bizarre horrors of our lives. We decided he would stay in the front room on the first floor. Despite being my brother, I chose to do not share any of the strange occurrences I had been experiencing in the house.

I figured that sooner or later, something would happen, whether to me or, worse, to him.

Once Alex finished unpacking, I suggested we take my motorcycle for a ride around the city's streets and avenues. The wind helped to clear my mind and distract me from the lingering questions about the spirits I was getting accustomed to coexist with.

At nightime, we returned to the house and I beggan to prepare a delicious dinner to celebrate my brother's visit. We then settled down to watch a movie on TV as part of a cozy evening at home. Before the movie even ended, we both began nodding off. Exhausted, we decided to head to our respective rooms and sleep.

The next morning, my brother explained to me his terrifying night with the spirits of the dead. He spoke with words full of fear, confusion, and concern. His nightmare began with a ghostly greeting whispered directly into his ear as he hovered between sleep and wakefulness. He mentioned that his rest was cut short when an unseen force yanked the sheets off his bed, leaving him exposed to the chilling cold.

To his misfortune, I was not the one pulling his sheets as a cruel joke, as he initially thought. To make matters worse, the relentless creaking of the old rocking chair began once again.

Reflecting on the events, I often think that his decision to run towards the source of the noise stemmed from a curiosity and intrigue that overpowered his mental and emotional limits, despite the prospect of facing an intense supernatural encounter.

When Alex reached the living room, he saw the rocking chair moving on its own, as if possessed. The atmosphere became dense and heavy, laden with sorrow.

He later described this moment as one of a paralyzing fear, which gripped his mind and instincts, except for the overpowering urge to flee. Instinctively, he ran to my room instead of his own, a decision I believe was no accident. He sought refuge and human company to cope with his turmoil.

His fetal position under my covers signaled the psychological and emotional distress he had endured. Although I knew he had experienced something, he chose not to tell me about it immediately upon seeking my company. In addition to the fear he experienced, he also mentioned seeing moving shadows throughout the house and hearing melancholic whispers that made it clear he was not alone. Rather, he was in the company of spiritual remnants bound to the house and its occupants. Fortunately, the paranormal events ceased for a while, allowing us to enjoy a few days of peace and happiness.

One warm afternoon, a kind elderly woman who was sewing and observing from her window greeted me cordially. Her polite demeanor and refined manners reminded me of old European aristocracy.

I returned her greeting, and we began a brief conversation during which she mentioned she often saw me coming and going from the house. She added that we had never had the chance to chat. During our pleasant exchange, she suddenly asked me:

—Have you ever been bothered while staying in that house?

I feigned ignorance, replying.

—I'm not sure what you mean. Could you clarify?

I hoped to extract more information about the house's history, but my ears trembled as she began narrating a story that defied civility and reason. She revealed the grim secret of the house, providing me at the same time with the answer to all the paranormal events taking place at the house. Its´s former owner was strangled to death by his own evil daughter, a heinous act motivated by greed, as she sought to claim her inheritance early, along with the family property and wealth.

The elderly woman ended her story by congratulating me for being the longest-standing resident in the house, noting that many others had come and gone but few dared to stay as long as I had. My resilience against the spirits evidently impressed her.

That same day, after learning about the house's dark history, the spiritual attacks escalated. My bed started to move violently as if it was being pushed by three people, unsettling me further. It seemed the spirits were disturbed by my presence and my newfound knowledge of their tragic past.

After yet another horrifying night, I eagerly awaited the morning to leave the house for good. I packed my belongings and, after a sleepless night, moved to a new residence at the Tropics Hotel.

Before departing, I thanked the elderly woman for her honesty and assistance. From this experience, I learned that spirits sometimes create strong bonds with a place, persons, or items and they remain unintentionally but persistently tied to the earthly plane, driven by unfulfilled desires or unresolved issues.Thankfully, my next residence was free of paranormal disturbances, allowing me to recover my peace and calm.

THE SUIT OF THE GHOSTLY PARTY

There was a time in my life when I began working in international tourism, which led me to travel from Belgium to the Dominican Republic to embark on a new stage in my professional career. I clearly remember being 23 years old, already more resilient in the face of paranormal events. This story unfolded when I was staying in a hotel room provided by the travel company that had hired me. When night fell and I was ready to sleep, during those delicate moments when humans relax and surrender to rest, an outrageous, wild, and loud party began in one of the finest suites the hotel had to offer, conveniently located right next to my room.

Each night became a constant source of frustration, as I couldn't get the rest I desperately needed to perform optimally in the tasks assigned by my bosses. During the day, it seemed as though no one occupied the Presidential Suite, but at night, it became the meeting place for a boisterous gathering. I could easily hear laughter, toasts, roaring cheers, and dances. As if sleepless nights weren't enough, another annoyance soon joined the nightly disturbances: someone began knocking on my door late into the night.

Believing it might be a hotel staff member or a lost guest confused about their room, I decided to turn the knob and open the door.

I found nothing but an empty hallway and faint voices from the ongoing party. I doubted anyone was deliberately trying to play cruel prank, so I dismissed the incident, thinking little of it.

One night at precisely 3:33 a.m., a notably eerie hour often associated with strange occurrences, the knocks came again, this time with more force. With this persistent, unwelcome visitor, my mood shifted to a more serious and cold state. When I got up to uncover the identity of this mysterious visitor, there was once again no one on the other side of the door. Only the unsettling and bizarre sensation of being watched lingered, as though something invisible was looking at me.

I returned to bed, irritated, trying to salvage what little rest remained of the night. I resolved to address the issue with the hotel managers the next day. This nightly partying and anonymous door-knocking had to stop.

The alarm rang the next morning, and after preparing myself, I went down to the reception desk to begin my inquiry. When I found the right personnel to address my concerns, I started a serious interrogation:

—Why do you allow such loud parties in the Presidential Suite every night? Don't you have any consideration for your guests?

—We're deeply sorry for any inconvenience, but no one is currently registered as a guest in that suite. And what you're describing isn't new to us, the situation has reached the point where staff only go up to that floor in case of a serious emergency.

Their tone and demeanor seemed to reflect the sincerity of their response, but I left the conversation dissatisfied and unsettled. Confused and intrigued, I returned to my room to gather my belongings for work. Later that day, I spent most of my time outside, attending to errands, making preparations, and holding meetings with clients to present details about the tour packages we offered.

That evening, when I returned to my room, words began to resonate around me:

—GET OUT OF HERE! LEAVE! LEAVE NOW!

These threatening words, spoken by some sort of spirit with no friendly intentions, significantly diminished my sense of comfort and trust in the hotel. After surviving that night of violent whispers from the restless spirits, I visited the reception again the following morning. I narrated in detail the horrors I had endured and followed up with a series of accusatory questions directed at the hotel staff. I noticed the manager's face hidding more information than they had disclosed earlier.

Sensing my mounting pressure, the manager eventually decided to be brutally honest. They offered to give me a tour to reveal the full truth and hopefully, put my mind at ease. As we walked, I realized we were heading toward the floor no one dared to visit.

After some conversation, we reached the Presidential Suite, where the manager pointed the source of the disturbance. The suite, they explained, had once been the favored retreat of Dominican Republic's former president, Rafael Leónidas Trujillo. It was where he frequently held gatherings with his most trusted ones. When we opened the doors, I was shown its full interior.

Upon entering, I confirmed that everything inside was of the highest luxury possible, from the nightstand to the dresser, to the coffee maker and the dining table, elegant chairs that matched the other furniture, paintings, and decorative items adorning the walls and shelves.

The suite's shelves brimmed with books and an array of ornaments, gave to the the room a presidential and executive ambience.

Once I learned the history and events tied to that suite, my desire to remain there transformed into an urgent and instinctive impulse to rent a house in the city and leave behind the attacks and discomforts caused by the festive spirits.

As I've shared before, there are many instances where the soul of a person becomes emotionally bound to a location, person, or object, manifesting itself in the physical world. In this particular situation, the nightly revelry seemed to recreate the enjoyment and celebratory spirit of Mr. Leónidas Trujillo during his prime years, centered in the suite he so frequently used for personal pleasure.

VANISHED THROUGH MY HANDS

I fondly recall an event as mysterious as it was thrilling, which took place one day when I decided to take a stroll through the streets of Puerto Plata, Dominican Republic. I was 21 years old, wandering through a distinguished plaza, enjoying the pleasant pedestrian atmosphere as I observed local shops, restaurants, souvenir stores, and clothing displays. For a brief moment, my attention shifted forward, and I noticed a very familiar person. My entire being filled with happiness and joy when I unexpectedly saw my mother. She stood amidst the bustling crowd, and at that moment, it had been quite some time since I had last seen her face in person.

After calming my emotions at the sight of her, my thoughts began to generate countless questions. Naturally, my immediate action was to run toward her and embrace her, eager to greet her and talk about things that only a mother and daughter could understand. As I approached, I called out to her from a distance, hoping to catch her attention, as her gaze seemed slightly unfocused and even distracted, My voice reached her, and she turned her head, looked at me, smiled, and then shifted her gaze back to where she had been looking before. It's important to emphasize how strange this was for me. After all, what mother, upon seeing her daughter after such a long time, wouldn't rush to greet her and embrace her as well?

Realizing she was walking away, I quickened my pace to catch up with her before she disappeared into the sea of people. Strangely, the distance between us seemed to stretch endlessly, no matter how fast I moved. Regrettably, I couldn't speak with her or embrace her, as just when my fingertips touched her right shoulder, what I believed to be her body vanished into the air like dense white smoke dispersing into the atmosphere. I was struck with great confusion and a slight fright, prompting me to head straight home to make an urgent phone call. My first thought was that something terrible might have happened to her, an accident or even a fatal calamity. The moment I entered the house, I rushed to the phone and, as quickly as I could, dialed her number, hoping she would answer and that no tragedy had occurred:

—Hello? Mom? Are you okay? I could have sworn I just saw you walking in front of me at the plaza, but something very strange happened when I touched you.

To this, she replied with a message that broadened my understanding of reality and the mysteries hidden within it:

—Hello, my daughter. A few minutes ago, I was sitting peacefully, praying, and thinking very deeply about you, missing you with all my heart, mind, and spirit.

After hearing her words, I sat on my bed to reflect on what had happened. I reached the definitive conclusion that, through some hidden mechanism, my mother had managed to transport her presence to a location near mine. I believe that by focusing her thoughts and emotions so intensely on me, she created an energy emission so strong and specific that it traveled a great distance and manifested as an unconscious projection, something that I would describe as a three-dimensional holographic silhouette shaped like her body.

KNOCKS FROM BEYOND THE GRAVE

On one occasion, an uninvited encounter occurred between me and the mystery of a cold night marked by an intrusive ghostly visit. I vividly recall, with great discomfort, how the door to my house fell victim to knocks filled with an ugly, repulsive dark energy, laden with hostile intentions and malevolent interests. A sudden and chilling tremor ran through my entire being, raising the hairs on my body and activating my fight-or-flight response against whatever might be lurking on the other side of the entrance door.

Although I initially felt overwhelmed, I decided to summon the courage to turn the knob and pull the door open. While no one was there, I couldn't shake the distinct feeling that something malevolent and sinister was prowling nearby. I made every effort to dismiss what had just happened and return to my sleepy state.

Approximately five minutes later, the knocks came again, this time louder and more insistent than before. It's worth noting that I wasn't expecting any visitors, especially not at such a late hour. My instincts warned me not to open the door, as the danger I might face could be far greater than I was prepared to handle at that moment.

Unable to sleep after the second round of knocks, curiosity got the better of me, and I decided to check if it might have been my neighbor needing something.

I put on my night robe and walked to her house. After ringing the doorbell, a sleepy woman opened the door. I said:

—Good evening, neighbor. I'm sorry to disturb your rest, but I need to ask. Have you by any chance knocked on my door recently? Or have you heard anything suspicious around the area?

—I'm sorry, dear, but I haven't heard any of the noises you mentioned. However, if you need anything, don't hesitate to call me again.

—Thank you so much, and I'm sorry again for disturbing you.

I returned home and went back to bed. Not even a moment had passed after resting my head on the pillow when I heard, for the last time, three knocks even louder, more violent, and more insistent than before. The horrific distinction this time was that, after the final knock, a chilling voice, the kind only a monster could produce, mockingly said:

—GOOD EVENING.

After the farewell from that spirit, the house grew cold rapidly and intensely, while a murky, malevolent energy took over the streets and rooftops, even unsettling the neighborhood dogs with fear and nervous agitation. Recognizing these signs, I understood that this dark entity wanted to make it clear that it was leaving to find more fear to feast upon elsewhere.

THE GIRL AT THE CEMENTERY

This event took place when I was 22 years old, during my time in Barahona, Dominican Republic. My coworkers and I were analyzing various tourist routes as part of the work assigned to us by the company we worked for. We were given a specific route and a special bus for our mission, with only the tour operators, the official driver, and myself on board.

After covering a significant portion of the route, near Lake Enriquillo, we witnessed a little girl wearing a white dress as she played among the tombstones and graves of a cemetery. As we passed by, the girl looked at us and waved, as if saying goodbye, while we continued our journey. We noticed there were no houses or buildings nearby, nor were there any other people in the area. This situation began to concern us regarding the girl's well-being.

Given these circumstances, we decided to turn back and learn more about her situation to offer any help she might need. When we arrived, the girl began to hide from us, almost as if inviting us to play with her. We were in a location miles away from any human building, and it was the middle of summer, with the temperature nearing 113 degrees fahrenheit.

The atmosphere grew increasingly unsettling. From the bus window, we asked her several questions, to which she only responded with a simple smile.

We assumed it was possible that a large family visiting the cemetery might have lost track of the girl while paying respects to a loved one.

Together, we carefully approached her position, but she began to move away, giving the impression she wanted us to participate in some kind of child's game. She hid and ran among the tombstones and graves. Despite her playful demeanor, as we followed her, we suddenly lost all visual trace of her movements, the last thing we saw being her hiding behind a tombstone.

Upon closer inspection, we realized it was pointless to try and find her, she was no longer there. However, her absence was replaced by an eerie, uncontrolled laughter that lingered in our ears for the rest of the day. It became clear that we were unprepared to deal with such circumstances. During the rest of the journey, we all maintained a long and collective silence.

Both the driver and my coworkers were as astonished and perplexed as I was, remaining in this state until we returned to the hotel. None of us have spoken of the incident since, but every time I approach a cemetery or see a girl in a white dress, memories of that chilling encounter with the beyond come flooding back to my mind.

THE HATMAN

Regarding my first direct experience with what is commonly known by names such as ghosts, the dead, or spirits of the departed, the initial contact occurred in my bedroom within the family home. In those moments of the night, the comforting memory of a warm dream where I fantasized about meadows bathed in the soft light of sunset was abruptly interrupted by the feeling that someone was there with me. The sensation of being watched was something I would describe as instinctive, intrinsic, and deeply rooted in my physical body. I knew I had to open my eyes to find out who the intruder was. Upon doing so, I observed a shadow beginning to form in one of the corners, near the night lamp on my right. The shadow advanced to the foot of the bed and started to take on a more defined and detailed shape, resembling what was onc a human being. Although its final form was that of a man wearing a hat on his head, I could not bring myself to fully believe what I was seeing. I had heard stories of people reporting sightings of ghosts in houses or cemeteries, but I had never experienced anything so direct.

This intruding man had already disturbed and interrupted many nights, leaving me in the grip of overwhelming panic, psychological shocks, and severe early-onset insomnia.

My parents were aware of what was happening to me every night, but whenever I ran to their room to explain the problem, they only responded with disbelief.

To them, it was nothing more significant than a recurring nightmare, incapable of causing such harm repeatedly.

Over time, I began to develop an understanding far beyond what a girl of my age could typically comprehend. With this newfound calm, I was better equipped to face that spirit, though I still harbored a trace of fear and respect for it, as its appearance bore a striking resemblance to that of my uncle Cisto. Many years passed, and by the time I was around eight years old, the mysterious man began to speak to me.

It was a tremendous surprise, but it did not distract me from his words, which carried a confession of regret and forgiveness. He revealed to me unprecedented and forgotten stories about the adventures of my family's ancestors.

Additionally, he explained that the primary reason he visited me was because I possessed the ability to see his spirit and interact with him both visually and audibly, although physical interactions were almost entirely excluded due to his electromagnetic composition and configuration.

Among all we discussed, one topic stood out, a matter I knew I needed to bring to my family's attention the next day. It would be a serious and challenging conversation, but ultimately, one that would prove healing and heartwarming. This peculiar and intimate spirit began to apologize for his wrongful behavior in the past toward my uncles and my father.

Up to that point, I had no knowledge of whether I had, or ever had, a grandfather on my father's side, as it seemed to be a complex and uncomfortable topic within our family, or at least among the adults. The next morning, I called for an impromptu family meeting to discuss the matter and bring us closer together.

I began by recounting my experience with the shadow that had been appearing in my room, as well as its true purpose in visiting me. I shared the impactful stories and messages that had been entrusted to me, including the important task of conveying a message intended to heal wounds that, for lack of understanding, had never been given the chance to mend.

The most crucial detail I could offer was that the grandfather wanted to ask for forgiveness from my uncles and my father for being so harsh and strict with them during their childhood. My story, delivered under their attentive gazes, stirred an emotional reaction in my father, bringing tears of sadness to his eyes—tears that seemed to belong to the child who had suffered during his early years.

In response to this extraordinary revelation, my mother revealed to me that the man who had been visiting me at night was, in fact, my grandfather, Gilberto Alfonso. After I shared the message with my family, the appearances of that soul ceased, though not without one final encounter.

On that last night, he appeared to me one more time, this time bathed in radiant, resplendent light that filled the entire room. It was his way of bidding me farewell before departing from this world forever.

NIGHTIME DEATH

I boarded a plane from France to the Dominican Republic with the mission of visiting my mother and the other members of my family. A few days after my arrival, my sister Elsa invited me to a party where friends and familiar relatives were gathering. Given the special occasion and considering the scorching heat that plagued those days, a large wooden table was set up, filled with a wide variety of drinks and delicious traditional Dominican food. Among all the drinks available, there were also many cans of beer, a liquid I had never drunk before, but, for my first time, it became something I allowed myself to enjoy.

I don't know if it was because the beer didn't have much alcohol, perhaps due to the food, or simply because my body tolerated it, but I was able to drink a lot without reaching the point of becoming dangerously intoxicated. Amid the laughter, singing, stories, dancing, and fun, the day came to an end, and the celebration was about to finish. My sister and I returned home, where my mother and my aunt Patria were waiting for us to sleep. Since there were many people in the family house, I had to share the bed with my mother. We exchanged goodnight and blessings before resting.

It wasn't long after we lay down when I began to feel the unpleasant sensation of suffocation that prevented me from thinking or calling for help, causing me great distress and discomfort.

The only thing my mind could do in that moment was issue a curious order to my soul. Although it may seem fantastical and unbelievable, I somehow managed to consciously leave my body. My spirit was compelled to move in order to escape the sudden and fatal lack of air, which was as lethal as it was painful.

Once outside, the sensation was one of strange and pleasant lightness, perceiving myself as a consciousness whose substance would be almost impossible to weigh due to its light composition. Although I couldn't see my body, I could feel it. Floating amidst the unknown, I was almost immediately transported in front of a cemetery. Despite the disorientation and the lingering memory of being lying next to my mother, I managed to spot some somewhat familiar silhouettes, which I recognized as my ancestors. It seemed that my ignorance of the situation evoked compassion in them, so they began speaking to me, telling me that my time to die had not yet arrived and that my presence there was unnecessary, urging me to return to where I had come from.

Gradually, I began to understand and accept that I had truly left my body, and that a different set of rules and norms governed that dimension, the one so often spoken of on Earth. After listening to them and accepting their advice, suddenly and almost instantaneously, I was transported back to my uncle Antonio's house. How did I know it was his house and not some other place? Simply because I saw him lying in his bedroom, peacefully sleeping with his wife.

It seemed that the material laws we are accustomed to in the three-dimensional world are different from those that exist beyond the confinement of matter. Slowly, I began to move through the house, including the room next to my uncle's, where his children were sleeping soundly.

After grasping the dimensional situation I found myself in, I recalled where my body was and the events that preceded the departure of my spirit. Before returning to it, I was engulfed by a distressing sense of despair.

Although the moments of that instant are not very clear due to the alteration caused by the shift in states of consciousness, I remember feeling intense pain in my chest and a great heaviness in my eyelids. With the little strength I had left, I opened my eyes and was met with the comforting and peaceful sight of my entire family surrounding me, while my mother on my left cried, prayed, and shook me, urging me to return to life. There was nothing more she could do in the face of such a sad reality. My entire body was cold, my skin pale with slight touches of purple, giving the impression that I had been exposed to an intense cold as freezing as death itself. I felt incomparable pain in my chest and extreme weakness. Additionally, my auditory perception was similar to hearing distant voices in slow motion, distorting my perception of the environment as if I were in a world almost unknown.

As is typical of a mother, her concern grew after noticing that my pale face revealed my true state of health. Without hesitation, she called for the others to bring an ambulance as soon as possible. During the wait for the doctors' arrival, the general worry of those around me slowly began to subside. The minutes felt endless until the medical assistance finally came. Once the paramedics arrived, they asked my family a few questions before performing an examination and diagnosis for my subsequent mobilization.

The destination was the emergency room, as the expressions of those attending to me revealed their concern, while they assessed my critical physical condition. Managing the situation with as much calm as I could muster, I passed through several rooms and machines that would perform a complete scan of my body's interior to precisely determine my condition.

After completing the necessary tests and all the required examinations, I was transferred to one of the hospital rooms where I would rest for the entire night. The doctor who attended to me, and who was in charge of my recovery, approached us with the results of all the tests and the final diagnosis.

In a serious yet kind tone, without hesitation, he told us that that night, while I was sleeping next to my mother, I suffered a pulmonary embolism that caused me to die for several minutes. After delivering these words, he proceeded to show us an image in which a wound in one of my lungs was clearly visible, confirming that I had died while sleeping.

DELIVERED FROM THE EVIL

Throughout my life, many moments of healing occurred. Cures and remedies of which I was a part and protagonist since my childhood, such as the case involving a young boy named Eddy, who was going through a very delicate health situation. He had a stomach condition that indicated the discomfort with which he lived. He appeared pale and bloated, something no child should ever suffer from. Despite numerous medical tests, they could never pinpoint the root of the problem. Although I was very young and had never received any medical training, I determined that Eddy was suffering from a parasitic infection, a problem nesting in his digestive system. Like Eddy, there are many people who suffer due to small, and sometimes not-so-small, creatures that live inside the body, causing widespread intoxication throughout all bodily systems due to parasites that hinder, contaminate, and consume.

Larvae and eggs are deposited in various places, while invading colonies seek to conquer the host body, where they also defecate and reproduce throughout the night. This is one of the reasons why many people cannot sleep and wake up in the early hours. Given that Eddy's condition was so extreme and painful, I decided to speak with his mother, Miss Tata, to let her know that I would be the one to heal him.

Eddy had to endure a severe illness for a long time, as many times he appeared in a critical state, but that was about to end. Thanks to the intuition I was born with, the necessary ingredients and the right preparation to achieve the healing effects of the components began to come to my mind. I had to make a tea with various herbs, spices, roots, and other natural products. Once prepared, rested, and strained, I served the tea in a cup to offer it to him. The moment he began drinking, all the parasites nesting inside him started to suffocate and paralyze, as they cannot survive in an alkaline and oxygenated environment. The tea I gave him served to counteract a tactic used by parasites: when they realize they are going to die, they begin to leave eggs behind, even releasing their waste before dying to spread toxins and filth as their last action.

The moment Eddy drank from the cup, the compounds and enzymes began to take effect, and just a few minutes later, he ran to the bathroom. After the unofficial therapy was over, each of us said our goodbyes and returned to our respective homes. The night passed without incident, until the next day, when the boy's mother came looking for me to talk. I thought that through her visit, my parents would find out about my therapeutic adventures and that I would be reprimanded with a severe punishment for taking such a risk without informing them in detail of the situation.

Much time had passed since Eddy's healing, and the people living in the surrounding neighborhood told me that the woman had always been very grateful for my help in healing her son, for now he was full of energy, vitality, and health.

THE APPARITION

When I was 9 years old, I went through a rather worrying phase in my life concerning a very close and beloved family member, someone I never thought we would one day find ourselves under totally anomalous and inexplicable conditions for the investigative lens of modern science. At that time, I was about to have a little sister with whom I could share and grow. Unfortunately, my mother experienced a sudden decline in health, worsening to the point where she urgently had to be taken to the hospital for the proper medical tests, to understand her health condition, and to take the necessary actions to ensure the well-being of both the baby and my mother. Several hours passed until the doctor in charge of her monitoring and review spoke with the family to explain her situation. After analyzing the tests, they diagnosed a small tumor near the baby's head. This was very bad news that shook us deeply, but not everything was lost.

The doctor recommended that the safest and most effective option would be to perform a surgical procedure to remove the small but problematic tumor. All the family members agreed to the surgery, placing their trust in the doctor and his specialized medical skills.

It's worth mentioning that I had no idea of my mother's actual condition, as being a small child, the adults thought it best to keep me ignorant of her state.

The day my mother went into surgery, my cousins, siblings, and I were at our maternal grandparents' house, from where we would leave to visit a river at the end of a long path through a beautiful botanical walk. We reached the river and began playing, joking, and making mischief, as only children can. The social laws were gone, replaced by the extravagant and pure energy of the here and now, which only a child can experience in what seems like a simple childish affair.

After a long time of fun and enjoying the fresh, pure air of the lush vegetation, clouds approached our location and positioned themselves right above our heads. The moment we began our walk back home, the water from the gray, low-hanging clouds started to pour down on us, changing the composition of the ground and turning the dry earth into dense, sticky mud. Accompanied by a downpour typical of the tropical climate in the Dominican Republic, we were almost at the door when the rain stopped, and the sun reappeared. Despite our filthy, muddy appearance, the children decided to keep playing in the grain dryer, messing around and creating things, while in the distance, I could hear my aunt Patria shouting for us to stop and clean up. Just as I was about to obey and go wash, I noticed that a familiar feminine silhouette began to materialize in front of me. As it gained more presence, it became easier for me to recognize it.

Before I realized it, the living reflection of my mother was standing before me, and I froze, gazing at her eyes filled with sadness. During the brief seconds that I locked eyes with her, my brother Alex noticed something strange and asked me:

—Are you okay? Do you need help?

Without taking my eyes off of where they were fixed, I quickly managed to say:

—Look, it's mom!

—Hmmm, that can't be. Maybe you're seeing her because you miss her a lot, remember she's in the hospital.

His words contradicted what I was seeing. I didn't know whether I could hug her or not, as I knew she was both there and not there at the same time, as her appearance resembled that of a digital hologram. Due to my strange behavior, Alex decided to come closer to me to give me a hug and comfort me. When he touched me, he was terrified and screamed loudly, for he had seen the presence of our mother. With fear in his body, he ran towards my aunt Patria, who was accompanied by my grandparents. My grandmother noticed our reaction and anxiety, so she asked what had happened to make Alex scream so alarmingly. Behind her, my grandfather Zenón spoke, a little annoyed by all the noise we were making in the grain dryer, finishing with a request for us to behave in a more proper and calm manner.

When we told them about the experience we had just had, they looked at each other with surprise and concern. Under those circumstances, they decided to reveal to us that our mother was in a delicate health condition after undergoing an important surgery.

Several days passed before my grandmother visited my mother after she had left intensive care. The surgery had been a success, and the doctor recommended she rest a few more days until she fully recovered and could return home.

After some conversation, my mother told my grandmother that something very strange had happened during the surgery, something very significant and special, with unforgettable details that would last forever, both in her mind and her heart.

Apparently, the place where her particular dream occurred was the same family house where my siblings, cousins, and I appeared covered in mud and playing together. This statement surprised my grandmother greatly, so she had to explain as best as she could that it hadn't been a dream, but my mother couldn't fully understand, especially due to the disorientation from the anesthesia.

This mysterious event was barely discussed, as it was a totally unknown topic and difficult for my family to comprehend, and it wasn't brought up again until December, when Alex confessed everything he had witnessed that afternoon with me. Although he was a witness, he never intended nor wanted to share his testimony of what had happened.

Several years passed, until one unexpected day, my mother called me to sit with her and discuss a topic that had been bothering her with curiosity for some time and that she needed to resolve. She told me very seriously that the day she was in surgery, she had a dream that seemed more real than reality itself. She shared with me in great detail the moment when she was able to observe us playing, while we ran around, scattering the mud with which we were covered. I wasn't surprised, but I was very intrigued to know that what my mother thought was a dream, was actually a journey of her spirit, a journey that her deepest feelings of love led her to experience in such a delicate and complex situation as one that occurs during surgery.

A CRY FOR HELP

During a period, I lived in the Dominican Republic while working in tourism at a very famous hotel in the country. While the job paid satisfactorily, there were days when I got home and the only thing I wanted was to sleep and rest. One of those nights, I had a torrid awakening after hearing one of the most chilling screams carrying my name. I'm not referring to the scream being terrifying in the sense of horror, but rather because that scream was asking for help and immediate assistance. I had a horrible premonition that something was wrong, especially when I realized that the scream sounded too much like my brother Alex's voice. I knew something had happened to him, and if it weren't serious, he wouldn't have called for help, so I got out of bed as fast as I could and quickly grabbed the phone to make an urgent call to check on his current state. Something in my heart told me he wasn't okay and that I had to help him however I could. Despite countless attempts to call his phone, there was no response from him. In this desperate situation, I had no choice but to leave the house, get in my car, and drive for 15 minutes to his residence, hoping to find out his whereabouts. I drove as fast and safely as I could within my driving skills until I reached his house.

I knocked on the door incessantly, hoping that he would answer and that the scream that woke me up had been nothing more than an unfortunate interruption caused by a nightmare.

Unfortunately, no one answered, which escalated my worry to overwhelming levels. I tried to calm myself as much as I could to think clearly and choose the best course of action from the limited options I had. The thought crossed my mind that maybe the neighbor knew where my brother was. I quickly went to the house next door and knocked on the door. Even though it was early in the morning, the lady agreed to answer my concerns:

—Good evening, ma'am. I apologize for interrupting your rest in such an unexpected way. I'm Carmen Baldera, Alex Baldera's sister, and I need to ask if you know where my brother is. I just knocked on his door, and it seems like he hasn't returned yet. Could you please help me?

—Hello, dear. Don't worry about waking me up. I know how much you love your brother. As for your question, the last time I saw him was when he left very early for work, but I never saw him return. This is all the information I can offer you. I'm sorry, but if I see him return, I'll be happy to let you know.

Tired of waiting and with my nerves somewhat calmed, I returned home to rest, carrying the hope that wherever he was, he was safe and out of any danger. Morning came, and I got up to start my daily preparation routine before work, when, unexpectedly, the phone rang. Something inside me told me that if I answered this call, I would finally know about Alex's situation.

After picking up the phone, a worker from a nearby hospital informed me that he had suffered an accident the previous night while driving on the road, and at that moment, he was hospitalized under medical supervision and care. When the call ended, I understood that the cry for help that had woken me up had come from my brother's soul, reaching out to me at the instant of the accident.

A VIOLENT DEPARTURE

Horror would sweep through one of the neighborhoods of South Tenerife, after the overwhelming and tragic news spread from mouth to mouth among the neighbors. I had no idea that the events of that day would be something that would break me emotionally and mentally far beyond anything I could ever have imagined. It was a summer day when the sun shone so intensely that even the neighbor across the street, with the fan on full blast, could feel himself almost cooking in the extreme heat. Despite the intense weather, that didn't stop my will to showcase the ultimate skill of my hairdressing and beauty expertise. Nothing that a couple of hair clips, a bottle of cold water, and the fan cooling the air couldn't fix. It was a longer day than usual, and just as I was closing the store, I felt an energy drop, signaling that it was time to take a few minutes to rest and recharge before returning to work in the afternoon. I only wanted to get home, but I knew I would need to prepare lunch for my son, so I was a little more patient with delaying the much-needed rest. As soon as I walked through the door, I got to work on lunch and, miracle of miracles, in less than thirteen minutes, I had set the table, prepared the meal, had the drinks ready, and washed the pots. After talking with my son for a moment and having lunch with him, I headed to my room, where all I wanted was to disconnect and relax.

By some strange luck, I managed to fall asleep almost immediately as soon as my head hit the pillow.

However, I was put on alert by a voice calling my name, causing a sudden awakening that pulled me out of my sleepy comfort. Gathering all my willpower, I focused more and more on the words I was hearing:

—Friend, I'm leaving! I didn't want to leave, but I am. It's my duty to go. It's no longer under my control!

I tried to understand the meaning of that message, somewhat confused by what had just happened. When I opened my eyes, I was stunned by the quick and fleeting image of a decapitated head bleeding, disturbing my mind and senses so much that I was forced to stay in bed for a long while to recover from the violent shock. The image lasted only a few seconds, but my shock didn't. Despite the unpleasant vision, I decided to dismiss the experience as something isolated that I shouldn't dwell on or give too much importance, so I could move forward with my work responsibilities that still awaited in the afternoon. Before heading to the shop, I called my friend Nina to come with me to work, not without telling her about the strange experience I had just had a few hours earlier while sleeping.

We agreed to meet at a specific point and headed in my car toward my hair salon to open up again. As we got closer to our destination, we began to notice the heavy presence of medical and police personnel in the area, so we decided to ask the officers what was happening and why access to the building had been restricted. In a very cordial manner, they informed us about the tragedy that had occurred in the apartment located in the same building as my shop.

A horrific murder had taken place that afternoon, where a man had been brutally and mercilessly decapitated, apparently as an act of revenge by an enemy. Upon hearing this news, the puzzle pieces fell into place, arranging themselves perfectly. The voice, the farewell, and the horrifying vision made sense to both Nina and me.

After looking at each other, we understood the truth of the events without needing to say a word to express our comprehension of what had happened. On that summer afternoon, my friend's soul chose to say goodbye to me, sending me the message of his final departure to the other side.

A SUDDEN LIGHT

This story took place during a time in my life when I worked conducting Tourist Operations at the Tropics Hotel in the city of Sosua, Puerto Plata, Dominican Republic.

At 19 years old, I witnessed a luminous apparition in front of my bed. It was a very ordinary night, and I was peacefully asleep, but a light illuminated my face so brightly that it nearly dazzled me, even with my eyelids closed, heavy from the deep sleep that consumed me. The sensation was very similar to when you close your eyes and someone shines a strong flashlight on you. I fought off the lingering drowsiness and opened my eyes to see how a silhouette of light began to take shape, resembling a little girl about 7 or 8 years old. Her entire being was made of a peculiar photonic glow that seemed to form her body while emanating light from within.

The mystery deepened with each passing moment, to the point where I stopped considering the impossibility of a child being in my room in the middle of the night, not to mention the fact that it was impossible for anyone to access my room without a copy of a key that I had never lent out. When our gazes met, we realized that we both recognized one another, though she recognized me far more than I could recognize her, of course. I began to feel a strange sensation in every cell of my being, as if I was or had been that little girl at some point in time.

It was a feeling that transcended all human logic, overwhelming me and coursing through every part of my being.

I was captivated by her fine details and delicate physical features, which gave her an immensely mystical aura. Her hair was styled in beautiful curls at the ends, and her skin was far paler than what is usual for most people. She had exceptionally light, bright brown eyes and exuded a charisma and nature that was humble, serene, innocent, and wise. As she began to move slowly and gracefully across the room, the light emanating from her body also moved across the walls, creating a unique, soothing, and comforting luminous atmosphere.

The recognition between us caused our gazes to remain locked the entire time. This state of awe continued for a few more minutes until the peculiar light emanating from her started to fade very slowly, and the corporeal form she had adopted began to dissolve like a column of smoke. Just as she had appeared, she disappeared, taking with her that beautiful and radiant magical light that had turned that night into something extraordinary.

I never understood why such a visit occurred, much less why she looked at me with that mysterious expression. Despite her great serenity, I felt as though, with her radiant eyes, she was trying to transfer the deepest secrets of her knowledge to me.

Perhaps it was some kind of warning or message, sent, who knows, from the beyond, the past, the future, or from some other unknown parallel universe.

Perhaps it came from an intricate web of energy connecting all paths, in all directions, in all moments, of all lives, across all worlds, of all universes that make up the multiverses of the omniverse, within the garden of God's house.

MY GRANDMOTHER'S MYSTICAL LIFE

To dive deeper and clearly investigate the reasons behind my distinctive traits and extraordinary abilities, it is necessary to understand the origin of the genetic inheritance passed down to me by my grandmother, Desideria Vélez Reynoso, through my mother. One must consider the human DNA's capacity to receive information from the environment and how all that collected data is transmitted to the next generation. This includes the transfer of knowledge, skills, and the corresponding human traits one inherits from their parents, who, in turn, received them from theirs.

My grandmother Desideria was an extraordinary woman, perpetually accompanied by an air of mystery throughout her life. A simple yet wise woman, she was special and enigmatic. She had a delicate and precise ability to predict future events, foreseeing them with days or even decades of anticipation. She could foresee who would visit her home on a given day and precisely how much food to prepare for them. Beyond these frequent and accurate predictions about visitors, she could also foresee the approximate date when a family member or friend might pass away, sometimes predicting this up to five days before it happened. Her ability allowed her to sense and even smell when death was approaching.

However, her abilities weren't solely focused on ominous events. She could also sense whether a pregnant woman would give birth to a boy or a girl and even predict if the newborn would have a long lifespan. Her powers allowed her to feel and perceive far beyond physical boundaries. She could sense and feel everything. If a neighbor was sad or lonely, she could feel their pain and would visit them to cheer them up. If someone had suffered an accident, she could sense it. Her powers were so remarkable that when someone entered her home, she could almost instantly discern what illness or discomfort they were experiencing, even if they showed no signs or symptoms of it. As a gesture of hospitality, she would suggest the herbs and flowers they should consume to recover and heal. If someone suffered from inflammation in a vital organ or any other form of cellular or metabolic dysfunction, she would detect it long before they visited a doctor. Many times, she even offered them the remedy they needed to restore their health.

She was particularly attentive to the less fortunate and those who needed help and care. Her kitchen was filled with jars containing various flowers, spices, leaves, and roots from which she extracted the active ingredients needed to treat the symptoms of what could be described as her "patients." She healed people. Some, under the veil of disbelief, dismissed the diagnoses she provided, while others, out of concern, would visit a doctor for a general check-up and later return, astonished, with confirmation that they were indeed ill. In many cases, those who ignored her warnings ended up worse off than they ever imagined. She never failed in a single diagnosis made with both heart and awareness.

Of all the things I could highlight about the time I spent with her, one of the most remarkable was her predictions about me and my future. She shared revelations about the distant historical events I would experience.

First, she examined the number of colors in my hair and, with great confidence and an assertive attitude, revealed the names of the countries I would visit during my life.

She claimed that the seven colors in my strands foretold that I would travel to a total of seven countries.

She also repeatedly emphasized that the problematic, conflictive, or distressing situations that people might cause me would serve only as opportunities to gain the necessary lessons for my maturity and evolution as a human being. Just as those people would act as teachers for me, I would eventually become a teacher for many others whom I had yet to meet. She explained that the pain others might cause me would serve to teach me the lessons that the path of life would lead me to discover.

On one particular occasion, she mentioned that I would live in "the center of the world," although I never truly understood what she meant. Despite being a woman who never received a formal education, an incredible incident occurred when my uncle Ramón Baldera was required to take a university test. However, an unfortunate leg injury had left him incapacitated during those days. The professor in charge of the subject asked a fellow student to deliver the sheets of questions to my uncle at home. Faced with the academic challenge, my uncle had no idea how to answer.

In response to this difficulty, my grandmother Desideria began dictating the correct answers under the astonished and attentive gaze of our family. One by one, she provided the appropriate responses, allowing my uncle to fill out all the exam sheets in record time. We were all shocked, as she had never studied under any academic institution, educational training, or literary guidance.

Days later, a letter arrived at the house notifying my uncle of his final grade on the exam. He was overjoyed to see that all the questions had been answered accurately and truthfully, earning him the highest possible score on a perfect exam. This incident only heightened the aura of mystery, wisdom, and magic surrounding my grandmother, increasing my curiosity and wonder about what other secrets she might share with me.

My interest grew so much that one day I decided to address a sensitive topic with her. Among all the things I remembered, there was one particularly distinctive feature about her: a strange scar on her leg. It was a mark that couldn't have been caused by a simple kitchen accident or an unexpected fall. This mark went beyond what we could categorize as something purely human. Although I had already heard the origin and story of such a mark, I decided to ask her directly:

> —Grandma, there's something I'd like to know, and I hope it doesn't make you uncomfortable. That scar on your leg, how did your skin end up like that? What happened to you?

She replied

> —One full-moon night, while I was in my room with the window open, a spectral apparition of a strange, luminous being resembling a firefly flew through the window and stood before me to make me a diabolical proposal.

From what I could gather, whatever this luminous being proposed must have been of significant importance but also dark and macabre, as she refused outright to carry out such malevolent and perverse acts that only depraved and merciless souls could conceive.

—Upon my refusal of the proposals from that glowing entity, I received a horrendous and violent blow, four fingers above my ankle, forcing me to sit on the floor while a cold sweat ran down my forehead from the pain, as I felt my bone nearly fracture. After that gesture, just as the firefly-like entity had entered, it left, while I remained on the ground, struggling to regain my breath."

The blow was so strong that it left a permanent mark, a lifelong reminder of that vile night of malevolent spirits spreading pain.

My grandfather recounted many strange and anomalous occurrences that were incomprehensible to anyone with even a passing interest in the paranormal. He described how, on several nights while sleeping next to my grandmother, she would inexplicably wake up completely soaked, as if she had gone to shower fully clothed and then returned to bed without drying or changing. In these unique circumstances, she would remain in a hybrid state of slumber and awareness.

According to her revelations, she claimed that on certain nights of certain months, a group of individuals would take her to a hidden waterfall where she had to travel through a path that granted access to an entryway concealed within the jungle. This entrance led to a secluded area inhabited by a civilization we consider extinct. This civilization, as she believed, was composed of Incas who were still alive and well. They shared mystical and ancient knowledge with her, teaching her secrets about life, the mysteries of the Sun, the secrets of the Moon, the true history of humanity, and countless other topics.

She was a generous, compassionate, and charitable person who never charged anyone for the help she provided.

Financially secure, she used her resources to assist others without hesitation. Alongside my grandfather, they legally owned several farms, a significant number of cattle, and many workers under their supervision. Of all her notable deeds, one of the most emblematic was her preparation of large pots of hot food to share with anyone who visited her. Her disinterest in money made her an even more genuine and advanced human being in terms of behavior and consciousness.

Eventually, the day came when her body reached the limit of its cellular regeneration. Her vital signs began to diminish alarmingly more than fifteen days before her passing. At that time, I was traveling but stopped my trip upon learning of her condition.

Before passing, she was bedridden for several days, showing signs that her time was running out. When I arrived in the town of Castillo, in the province of Duarte, everyone made way for me as I headed toward her house. Upon arriving, I saw a crowd of people, which frightened me as I feared the worst.

Upon entering her home, I saw her surrounded by many deeply saddened family members. She had not opened her eyes for ten days. Still, some kind of force kept her breathing through a fragile thread of air. Slowly approaching her, I delicately held her feet with love. As I stood close to her, I heard what is known as the sound of death, a faint exhale from her nose, followed by a pause. With wide eyes, she looked at me and gifted me her final smile. She displayed one last expression of joy at seeing what she loved most on this earth one last time, a little girl she once called "my little one."

Our eyes met for a few fleeting seconds before she slowly closed hers and sank back into the pillows. Her breathing ceased, followed by the stillness of her heart.

On the day of her passing, the street where her house was located had to be closed to vehicles due to the overwhelming number of people who came to bid farewell. Friends, neighbors, and relatives poured in, exceeding what a funeral parlor could accommodate. Thus, we decided to hold the wake at her home until it was time for her burial.

Vast and numerous was the number of neighbors, friends, and relatives who gathered that day just to bid their final farewell to a woman who left a lasting mark on their lives. Her legacy imparted great lessons and cherished memories to others, thus managing to illuminate a part of the world with the light she carried in her noble heart.

AN UNEXPECTED VISIT

It was a calm and serene night, filled with an array of colorful dreams, until I woke up disturbed by the feeling of an intruder in my room. At 23 years old, I had never felt a presence so familiar yet so strange, as if the vague memory of past lives clouded my mind and my present. I knew the observer was very close to my bed, leaving me with only two options: to stay under the covers, hoping it would disappear in the face of my feigned absence, or to gather enough courage to confront it.

The air grew heavy with a sinister energy that filled every corner of the room. I took a deep breath and prepared myself as best I could to face it. The depictions I had seen of its likeness were completely accurate. Before me stood the very embodiment of death, the entity we call Death. At times, I wavered between believing what I was seeing and hoping that I would soon wake up, startled, from this dream. But as the seconds passed, I adopted a calmer and more serene state of mind.

She was towering, draped in tattered garments made of worn fabrics, the edges of which emitted a faint gray mist, resembling a dense vapor that envelops the figure of one who symbolizes the end of life on Earth.

Though she had no face, I could sense that she was experiencing what humans call sadness. Despite the absence of eyes or eyebrows, I felt her state was one of sorrow and regret.

The thought crossed my mind that one of my relatives might soon pass away. For the entire time she stood before me, I remained seated on my bed, observing her intently and with curiosity, while my mind wandered with questions and doubts, imagined scenarios, and wild theories. After a long twenty minutes, I began to hear the distinct sound of a landline telephone ringing in the distance. The sound itself didn't frighten me, but the idea that behind that call might lie terrible news unsettled my senses and threatened to ruin my night.

I ran as fast as my pajamas would allow and picked up the phone with curiosity. Sadly, I was met with a series of cries so piercing they could split the heavens. Only a mother suffering in her soul could wail such anguished and harrowing cries of pain over the loss of her beloved young son, whose death had occurred just minutes earlier. I could hardly believe her words. It was all so strange to me, especially since I had spoken to him that same afternoon through an international phone call just to say hello.

I did everything I could to console her and support her as she navigated the pain and loss of someone so precious. I asked her to tell me the cause of his death and the circumstances surrounding those fateful moments. As she began to recount the events, my sadness deepened, and I was overwhelmed by an apocalyptic wave of despair and distress. The child had been staying at his grandparents' house, where he lived with a large and kind dog he had grown deeply attached to.

That night, he was eager for the dog to join him in bed as he slept. However, his grandfather had very strict rules about allowing animals inside the house.

This conflict of interests escalated into a heated argument, so loud and intense that the boy suffered a severe asthma attack due to heightened nervous agitation.

My first reaction was denial, but I eventually came to terms with the situation and understood why I had received such a strange visit. After finishing my conversation with my friend, I called her parents to offer my condolences for the tragic incident. That night marked the first time in my life that Death visited me to warn me that someone I knew was about to depart.

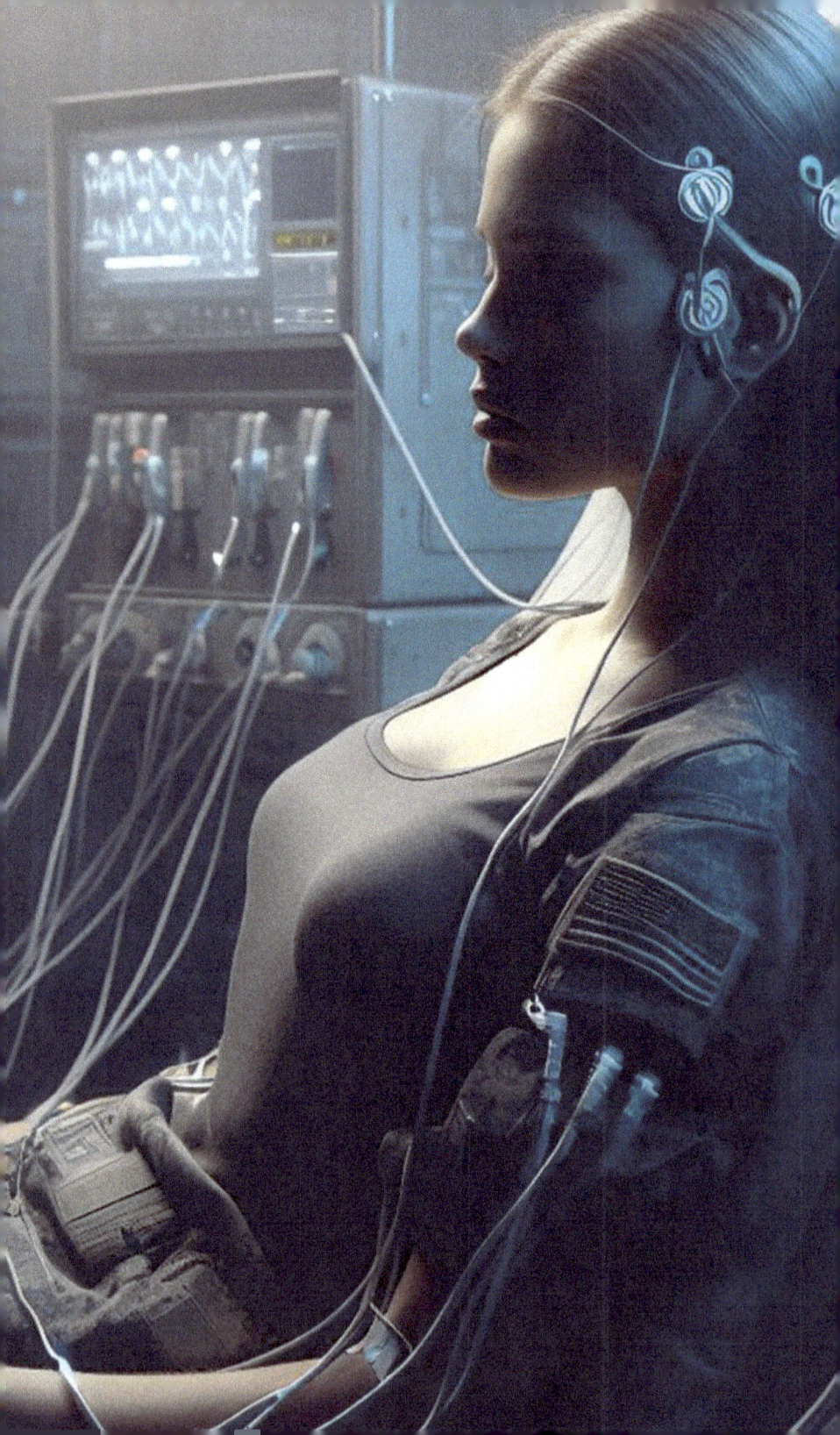

STUDIES IN THE DREAM UNIT

There is a particular story that intertwines medical science and the paranormal world. At that time, I was undergoing various medical exams and tests, both neurological and cardiovascular, as part of an investigative review to uncover the reasons behind the many mysteries within me. During one of the numerous analyses, several doctors discovered a cerebral anomaly that stood out in the results. Initially, I was diagnosed with a small tumor in one of the examined areas. However, this diagnosis was quickly corrected by another doctor who realized that what they thought was a tumor was, in fact, my pineal gland, which was exceptionally developed.

The size of a typical pineal gland is comparable to a tiny lentil seed, whereas mine is larger than a chickpea. Among other things they were studying, they were also trying to determine why my nightly sleep duration ranged from just ten minutes to a maximum of two hours. Few people know the feeling of hardly sleeping and even less so of not truly resting, which I attribute to my heightened ability to receive frequencies.It is essential to emphasize the significance of the pineal gland in the realm of mystery, as it allows the reception of various frequency waves that our eyes cannot detect, thus reflecting and revealing things beyond the physical scene and dimension.

We must remember that our perception is limited by the five senses we use to interact with the world at all times.

This type of dimensional interaction occurred one particular night when I was in a special sleep unit, filled with all kinds of instruments, machinery, vital sign monitors, scanners, cables, and many inquisitive eyes waiting for something extraordinary to happen. Luckily for them, that very night, as I lay on the bed, I began to notice an increase in visits from the spirits of the deceased.

Little by little, a multitude of visitors from the beyond started arriving, attempting to contact me for various purposes. Some asked me to deliver a message to a loved one on their behalf, others were lost and disoriented, seeking guidance, and others simply visited because they were aware that my ability to see them was unique. They saw my gift as a bridge between their world and the living.

Despite the overwhelming spiritual visits, I chose not to confess to the doctors or scientists what I had seen, as there was a high likelihood they would diagnose me with hallucinations or temporary insanity. The researchers asked if I had seen or felt anything, to which I replied that I hadn't seen anything and that no anomalous event had occurred in the testing room. Following my statement, they decided to show me a video that was both astonishing and impactful.

During the night, they had placed an infrared camera to capture a different spectrum of electromagnetic waves. The footage revealed the forms, visits, and presences of the spirits moving around me, making it evident that I could no longer hide the experience I had truly lived.

With speed and precision, they began to write down observations about what had been recorded. However, there was one doctor who remained skeptical.

He was a man deeply resistant to paranormal topics, but his entire belief system collapsed at the exact moment I began to tell him that the immense suffering he was carrying needed to be released and resolved.

With great respect, I spoke to him about how and under what circumstances his beloved mother had passed away. She had asked me to deliver a message to her son as her final wish, confirming for his scientific mind the existence of other dimensions. He was deeply shaken, especially since that sensitive topic was something he had never discussed with anyone, not even his family or colleagues.

MIRACLES OF FASTING

Following the medical theme, this story involves a very peculiar and distinguished test, one that most people would think twice about before attempting. Despite being a relatively simple challenge, the psychological difficulty was so high that the average person would find it hard to succeed. My task was to abstain from consuming food for ninety days to observe how my body would react.

I had met some special doctors who became interested in me, and after a long conversation in which I answered a series of questions honestly, they eventually informed me that I had the capacity to live without human nutritional sustenance, relying instead on the intake of cosmic energy from the universe.

Since I had never attempted such a feat before, I felt somewhat nervous and worried about what might happen to me. It's important to note that my daily metabolic progress and health status were constantly monitored by the doctors, and any significant changes I experienced throughout the day had to be reported to the medical research center.

Given the psychological weight of the test, I feared that my hair might start falling out due to the lack of food.

To my surprise, however, interesting things occurred throughout the detoxification process that fasting entails.

To begin with, my colon underwent a spectacular cleanse, as did my small and large intestines, which also became purified.

As part of the test, I was asked not to use deodorant during the ninety days to check if my body would produce any unpleasant odors. Amazingly, I had no body odor whatsoever, and even though I did not brush my teeth, I did not develop halitosis or any oral health issues. My overall health was excellent, and my physical condition was flawless.

At the start of the experiment, I was fearful of not eating, so I asked the researchers if I could consume a minimal amount of food during the initial days. We agreed that I would only consume one mint leaf, three almonds, and a cup of green tea. There were no breakfasts, lunches, or dinners for me during that time.

During the first three to five days, I experienced extreme physical weakness, just climbing a staircase would leave me completely drained. However, in the days that followed, I began to notice an unprecedented surge of energy and enthusiasm in my life. I had never felt so happy or so physically strong.

Sometimes, I would go to the beach to watch the waves and walk for hours. Afterward, I would climb La Montaña Roja (The Red Mountain), located on the southern coast of Tenerife in the Canary Islands, Spain. Initially, I would ascend the mountain over the course of two hours, almost running.

Eventually, my energy levels became so elevated that I could run up the mountain at full speed without succumbing to exhaustion.

All these experiences demonstrated to me the value and power of fasting. While the results were incredibly promising, after the ninety days had passed, I received a message asking whether I wanted to continue the experiment or return to my traditional eating habits.

I decided to return to my old way of eating. It was a personal pleasure for me to share meals with friends whenever I visited a restaurant to sing. On many occasions, after performing, the restaurant owner himself would cover the bill.

A WARNING FROM BEYOND

At the age of 20, I found myself traveling on a highly comfortable airplane from Quebec, Canada, to my homeland, the Dominican Republic. Upon arriving, I decided to rent a large house with impressive architectural dimensions and stunning aesthetic features. This house boasted a beautiful and magnificent garden, yet strangely, there were no roses planted anywhere, a rather intriguing detail, given that each day the unmistakable scent of countless roses began to fill the air.

The aroma was so strong and pervasive that it felt as though roses were growing in every corner of the property, both inside and out. This exceptional event always took place at dusk, with the rich fragrance appearing and disappearing intermittently.

After spending a few days in the house, I had to stay alone in that enormous property. To add to the predicament, the person responsible for cleaning and maintaining the house would be absent over the weekend to visit family in another city.

As night fell, I retreated to my room to organize a few things and rest.

Just as I was about to wrap myself in blankets and start my nightly reading session, the silhouette of a man suddenly appeared, delivering a warning:

—Be careful! Watch out! You must be careful!

Moments after this sudden apparition, and before even a few seconds had passed, I began to hear noises coming from the lower floor of the house. Chairs and various pieces of furniture were being dragged across the living room and kitchen floors. It became clear to me that intruders had broken into the house with the intent of stealing, as the noises revealed they had breached the property's security perimeter.

In those circumstances, my only option was to reach for the phone on my bedside table and call my neighbor, who, fortunately, was at home. In a hushed tone, with minimal vocal effort, I informed her of what was happening:

—Neighbor, some people have broken into the house, and I think they're robbing me.

She understood immediately. Within seconds of our conversation, her son stepped outside, positioned himself a few meters from their house's entrance, and fired two warning shots into the air with his pistol.

The intruders fled in terror, running as fast as they could in the opposite direction of the gunshots. According to investigations conducted by the police, it was determined that the crime had been carried out by four individuals, based on the footprints and their distribution, along with other scene-related evidence.

To this day, I don't know who the man was that warned me that night with his message of caution.

He could have been someone who had lived in that house and passed away, or perhaps an ancestor I never had the chance to meet. He might have even been some type of guardian spirit.

What I do know is that he had been human at some point in his life, as his aura and energy were different from those of ascended beings, who possess a distinct type of light and presence. In any case, just as suddenly as he appeared, he disappeared, and I have never seen him again.

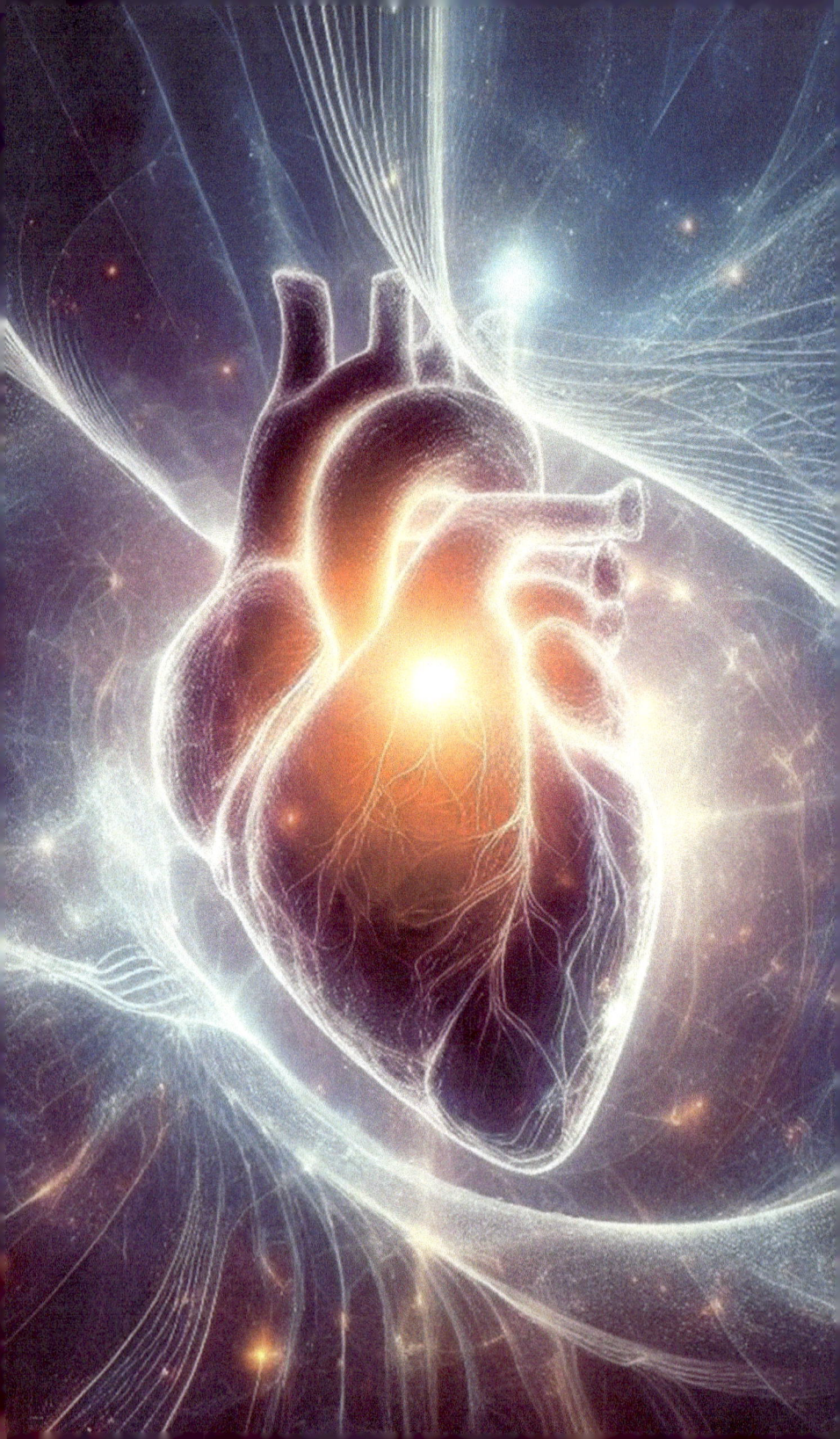

HEARTH COMPLICATIONS

Among all the experiences I can share, one of them is related to investigative medical science. My initial encounters with this branch of human knowledge arose from various physical conditions deeply rooted in my body. Through multiple studies to which I was subjected, blood tests, genetic laboratory analyses, saliva sampling, medical check-ups, and inquiries from doctors regarding my feelings and pain, it became evident that my ailments stemmed from my heart, which was distinguished by having a unique cardiac pathology.

I lived under the constant shadow of suffering from extremely severe headaches, high blood pressure, extreme fatigue, and the dreadful sensation of collapsing, feeling as if I might die at any moment with my chest tight and suffocated.

This problem was not new; I had suffered from heart issues since childhood. However, these sensations were things I could not articulate clearly enough to receive urgent and immediate care or the treatment I needed at the time. Decades later, I came to understand various aspects of my current life and how they were inexorably interconnected with other past lives, separated by space and time.

Gradually, and through different visions and revelations, I discovered that my afflictions and fears originated from traumas related to my deaths in previous incarnations, during eras and civilizations that are now history and remain stored in the planet's memory.

I have walked this Earth in various settings alongside a multitude of historical and lesser-known figures, during times marked by violence. Hundreds of years ago, in the harsh lands of Europe, humanity was clawing its way back from near extinction. These were bleak times in remote cities of what we now call France, where evil roamed freely, traveling from village to village, from city to city, attacking and consuming everything in its path.

A war had broken out against reddish and grayish beings with tough, cold skin. These creatures bore emblems of evil and thrived in dark corners. Malevolent in nature and with bloodthirsty intentions, they flew and patrolled the skies, waiting for the right moment to carry out their cruel raids.

Standing against them were the Wise Ones, who possessed power and complete protection against the creatures. They dwelled in the mountains, a sanctuary where they guarded their teachings and secrets. Their oldest manuscripts contained drawings of these beings, detailing their origins and the ways to defeat them. The creatures' physical characteristics were recorded with meticulous detail, making their appearance well-known, especially to those who had seen them up close. Unfortunately, few survived such encounters.

Some children who managed to escape would describe, with difficulty, the creatures' appearance and the horrific way people were crushed, dismembered, and consumed in a whirlwind of blood, violence, and sadism, reaching a level of depravity that only a spirit from the underworld could conceive so diabolically.

The creatures' black horns, protruding from their heads, marked their infernal nature. Their wings, attached to their backs, were made of membranous flesh, and they had massive hands with filthy, greenish-yellow clawed fingers. The scenes recounted by survivors are fleeting and fragmented in their memory, considering that the terror of the moment suppresses both thought and reason.

To face them, I had access to a vast arsenal provided through multiple connections within the administration of the Council of Wise Ones. At my disposal were all kinds of weapons I could need, including tactical combat gear, specialized war knives, steel-toed waterproof mountain boots, a titanium mesh vest, multiple poisoned daggers, a short sword, a long sword, a crossbow with a three-hundred-arrow magazine, smoke grenades, distraction grenades, and a secret sacred weapon. My will and determination were strong enough to endure all the adversities and hardships that plagued the city. The scourge of the flying devourers had begun to spread across Europe, leaving as the only deterrent a small contingent of members from the Special Forces of the Final Response Unit. They worked as a team to halt the advance of those hordes, which I had once been their destroyer. I was the fear that those who instill fear dreaded. The declaration of war was clear, and my will and judgment were ready for battle. Although the puzzle lacks the necessary pieces to complete the entire picture of the timeline, due to historical omissions over decades, centuries, and millennia, you can still see, from a distance, the image of what was and who I was.

The most memorable moment I carried with me was the instant of my death in the midst of a violent fight. I fell to the ground, a victim of a fatal wound to my heart caused by the tip of an enemy's cursed and enchanted spear. It had pierced through my armor, fatally wounding me and thus ending my experience of life in that era. It is worth noting that multiple past lives can have soul connections to this current life, manifesting through various unconscious psychological configurations.

For example, my fear of the ocean is something I still find difficult to confront and manage. The indelible and vivid memory of what was once one of the most traumatic experiences for any being on Earth still lingers in the deepest recesses of my unconscious mind. In Atlantis, we enjoyed what, compared to our current modern science, would be considered magic rather than technology.

We traveled using highly advanced personal crafts, remarkable in their design and functionality. We had technological and linguistic advancements in fields such as galactic computing. It was an era when the general sentiment and attitude of society was one of historical immortality, as though our civilization was destined to prevail against the passage of time. However, our arrogance and hubris began to pose a threat to ourselves and the planet, as the pursuit of technological and scientific conquest drove us further away from our true selves.

Despite collectively enjoying long and prosperous lives, our interests veered toward sinister and self-serving goals. There were disputes and conflicts, greed and deceit, great societal unrest, and chaos in the civil order. On the fateful dark day, our consciousness was shaken by the onset of a war that spread across the entire territory known as Atlantis. Authority had become corrupt, and the discord among factions and groups was palpable.

But we had no idea that the truly horrifying was yet to come, reaching us in an unexpected and catastrophic manner.

Etched into my soul is the dreadful, terrifying memory of that colossal tsunami, towering and destructive, relentlessly advancing toward the continent's shores. Its sheer presence marked the destiny that awaited us all. Though some tried to escape in any way they could, that monstrous force of the sea knew neither mercy nor compassion.

Everything it touched with its waters was forever buried under the drenched and chaotic remnants of what was once our home, our legacy, and our history.

As various pieces of the puzzle of my story as a human being were revealed to me, I began to gain a better perspective and a deeper understanding of the physical and psychological ailments I experienced and their connection to past-life experiences.

On multiple occasions, I have woken up distressed and almost unable to breathe after dreaming about an intense scene from a previous life. Sometimes, I received information through dreams, and at other times through visions. In one particular revelation, I saw a medieval city where people would often become aggressive, judge without justice, and kill collectively.

During medieval times, witch hunts and the persecution of people with doctrines, practices, rituals, and traditions different from those promoted by the Inquisition took place in broad daylight. Tragically, under the authoritarian standards of that era, anyone could become a suspect. I was fully aware that I was risking confrontation with a brutal and violent enemy if my work and the materials I crafted at home were ever discovered.

I worked with various herbal preparations and natural macerations, which I used to heal and treat people. The townsfolk knew of my knowledge and sought my help to alleviate the ailments that afflicted them unexpectedly. I had improved the conditions of many patients and healed countless others, but I should have known that such activities could not continue for much longer. The persecution, accusations, trials, and burnings of so-called witches had increased significantly in the past months.

Everything was going well until a malicious, envious person accused me of acts and deeds in which I had never taken part. Many people had tried to uncover my recipes and mixtures, but that woman knew I would never reveal them despite her previous attempts at spying, disguised as friendship. I was accused of conducting rituals, practices, and concocting potions of magic and witchcraft in my home, allegedly poisoning and addicting the people who sought my help. She also accused me of performing dark evocations with dead languages and strange chants that scared away crows and stirred flies into motion.

Faced with these grave and horrific accusations, the local officials and neighbors decided that the best way to verify her claims was to raid my home and search for magical instruments and forbidden books containing pagan texts of outlawed cults. Unfortunately, at the time, I had a shelf filled with various glass jars containing multiple compounds, each labeled with its name, usage instructions, and the ingredients used in its creation.

It didn't take long for them to arrive at an inhumane conclusion, where the innocence of an individual was not even considered worthy of proper investigative scrutiny.

They decided that the best way to determine whether my words about my human nature, and not that of a witch, were true was through the brutal and sadistic test of burning me alive in front of the watchful eyes and gossip of the townsfolk. My sentence was set, and while my conscience was clear, I felt saddened by the ignorant hysteria born from the minds of people of that era.

Truth be told, many of my friends had been burned before me. After being apprehended, I was taken to the center of the village, where a wooden post and ropes had already been prepared to tie me and begin my judgment.

Confronted with the prospect of being burned alive, I suffered a severe nervous breakdown, to the point of fainting and losing consciousness.

After that, I left my body and witnessed in third person how the flames rose and consumed what I once was.

EXTRATERRESTRIAL CONTACT

It was an October night in 1999, and I was peacefully lying in bed, sound asleep, wrapped up warmly in my bedroom. It had been a tough day, and I needed rest and well-deserved sleep, which was violently disrupted by a horrifying pain I had never experienced in my entire life. The pain came from the area corresponding to my right ovary, in my lower abdomen.

When I managed to open my eyes, struggling through the agony, I realized my legs were hanging off the edge of the bed, adopting a rather uncomfortable position for any woman. To my dismay, the reason for my strange bodily posture was not because I had moved during sleep or wandered through some idyllic dream. It was due to the physical manipulation of those small, bald, gray-skinned beings positioned in front of me.

What I was witnessing was so terrifying that an experience like this would leave disturbing memories in anyone's mind for a lifetime, as it has in my case. Those beings, with large eyes and small mouths, were performing an extraterrestrial insemination on me. If this is the first time you've heard this term, you might not be familiar with the fact that there are people who have been used as incubators for extraterrestrial beings for various paranormal, military, and scientific purposes.

I knew I was awake because I could clearly hear the cars passing by on the street, and the pain I was experiencing provided undeniable confirmation that it was all real, though I always wished it wasn't. The terror was so overwhelming that I couldn't move or speak, going through something akin to undergoing surgery while fully awake, without anesthesia.

There was a moment when I made eye contact for a second with several of the extraterrestrials. They noticed my conscious state, realizing that I wasn't under the supposed anesthetic state they believed I was in. However, they didn't seem to care that I was watching them, as they continued with their task nonchalantly.

Gathering all my lucidity, I managed to count up to five aliens inside my room, of which only one was "operating" on me. Two were standing beside it, while another two were positioned a bit farther from the surgical area, as if they were guarding the surroundings. The psychological impact was so immense that my anguish and distress made me feel an uncontrollable need to scream desperately, but I couldn't. Once they finished their abnormal procedures, they vanished from my sight. During the intrusion, I was wearing a white nightgown, which had been stained with a significant amount of blood from a wound I couldn't locate. There was no scratch or visible cut anywhere on my body to suggest that it had been manipulated in any way. For the next five minutes after their visit, I was unable to move due to the lingering pain caused by the extraterrestrial medical activities performed on me.

When I could finally get up, I dragged myself to the shower and checked if I might have been on my period to explain the bloodstains. In the days that followed, my nights turned into episodes of anxiety, fear, and terror at the thought of their potential return to my home, leaving me unable to sleep for many weeks.

After that first night, my abdomen began to swell in such a strange way that I went to see a doctor for a medical examination.

The doctor, however, attributed what I had experienced to a state of partial somnolence and prescribed me some pills to calm my nerves as a solution. The assistance I received didn't help much in resolving the mysteries swirling in my head, nor did it soothe my emotional and psychological instability. Although I wasn't pregnant at that time, the swelling in my abdomen reached such an extent that, by the time I realized the situation, I had to buy new clothes and get rid of the ones I was wearing. My astonishment at the growth of my abdomen was so great that I decided to weigh myself on the scale, only to discover that I had gained 14 kilograms of body weight.

Living in this strange condition and after approximately four months, my abdomen suddenly returned to its normal state overnight without me noticing any sign of expelling whatever had been growing inside me. Seasons passed, years went by, and I continued to wonder what it was that had been gestating within me.

At that time, I had no knowledge or reference to help me identify or categorize those beings that we now call Greys, Aliens, or Beings from Space. I didn't know who they were or what their intentions were with me. Under this premise, a significant amount of time had to pass before I could learn about their story. For years, I questioned that unfortunate night every single day.

I lived without answers to basic and essential questions such as: Who were they? What did they want? Where did they come from, and how long have they been here? Nearly on the brink of despair and saddened by my inability to satisfy my curiosity, the day finally came when I would get answers to my questions. By chance, I opened a magazine and, on one of its many pages, I found a small section characterized by a peculiar drawing.

The graphic representation was strikingly similar to the beings I had seen that night.

It turned out that they were the so-called Greys. Upon seeing such a similarity, I suffered a momentary shock that forced me to sit down in a chair.

I began to tremble while my gaze wandered into the well of past memories, recalling an event I had never spoken of, and several tears began to slide down my face.

Gradually, over time, I started to forget that period of my life and began moving toward new projects and relationships in my social environment. More than a decade and a half had passed until, one day in 2016, while I was rehearsing some songs with a great friend and professional musician, I experienced a sudden vision of images that began materializing while I lost track of time and space. Before me appeared three Greys, accompanied by a smaller one, with features somewhat different from the others. The less developed Grey had the physical appearance of what we might categorize as a humanoid teenager, around 16 years old. This time, I wasn't scared; I stayed still and calm, while the largest of those beings began to communicate with me telepathically:

—We have come so you can meet your son.

—What do you mean? How is his is going to be my son!?

—Don't say that. Please respect us. We have planted our seed in you, as our reproductive abilities are no longer available to us due to the genetic modifications we underwent long ago.

I understood that this is one of the reasons why they carry out abductions around the world using matter-manipulating technology. Astonished, I watched that being with great attention to everything it communicated to me.

—Although some of you label us as evil and dark, in this case, it's like with humans; there are all kinds of people, both hostile and benevolent.

—Well, you are not so good, because ever since you performed that insemination on me, I've been experiencing a lot of pain and issues with my menstruation. What have you done to me?

—We would like to apologize for all the discomfort and pain we have caused you, but the real reason for our visit is because your extraterrestrial child was eager to meet you. I also must thank you, as the universe needs more benevolent people like you, and what you have done has helped create a new beginning for us and our species. He does not have attachment to you and is somewhat different from us.

I've done a lot of research on certain unofficial topics, and it turns out that there are beings who have the ability to control matter at will, pass through walls and ceilings, make objects appear and disappear, create dimensional manipulation cubes, project images and voices into people's heads, paralyze bodies, and do other things.

This has been the greatest horror and pain I have ever experienced, pain that even to this day is difficult for me to express and talk about. Because of the trauma caused, it's been a hard task for me to reveal these details.

At some point, I would like to undergo a regression to see what really happened when I was asleep and unaware of an alien presence in my room. Since that contact, my lymphatic drainage has never been the same. Even today, I feel like my body remains out of balance.

Since I was revealed the existence of a hybrid child, I've often thought about all that we don't know about the beings that inhabit the universe, and how the vastness of existence is something that escapes our limited earthly understanding.

TENSHI

It was the final days of January 2014, on the island of Santa Cruz de Tenerife, Spain, at a time when I had the task of going to a residence where two elderly gentlemen were waiting for me to cut their hair, a task I had to carry out at the end of each month. After finishing my work, I was about to get into my car with the intention of driving back home. During the journey, I noticed a young man, around thirty to thirty-four years old, signaling to me as if he wanted me to stop. He was wearing a striking light blue suit of high quality, which was likely very expensive. Standing over 190 centimeters tall, he had an elegant posture, and his presence exuded magnanimity.

He possessed a dazzling beauty, radiating an aura of peace and harmony that I had never sensed in anyone else. It gave me a feeling similar to the one experienced when observing a beautiful meadow filled with wildflowers of all colors and species, beauty that transcended the limits of physical matter. I'm not used to stopping for hitchhikers on the road, but with this man, I felt that nothing bad would happen if I picked him up. As I approached his position, I began to slow down until I finally stopped right in front of him.

—Good afternoon, where are you going?

—I'm going wherever you go.

I told him I was heading to San Isidro, but he didn't seem to care much. I thought he might be traveling to El Médano. After signaling for him to get into the back of the car, he entered, and I began to perceive a curious scent of flowers and roses, as if a mix of natural aromas had taken place, filling the air with a sweet, yet citrusy perfume, with refreshing notes similar to morning dew. Amid the overwhelming fragrance and my delight in it, I almost forgot to respond to the greeting he gave me when he got in the car.

Along with the floral smell, I also felt a curious sense of calm, peace, and extraordinary well-being. Just his mere presence gave me a feeling of deep familiarity, as if I hadn't seen him in a very long time, even though I didn't know him at all. Suddenly, he began to tell me very curious and particular things about me, so during the rest of the ride, we had a conversation that I will try to recreate from memory with as much detail as possible:

—Never change. Always be yourself at all times. Never let the circumstances of life change you, because people like you are rare in this world. In this life, keep being who you are. Keep helping others.

—Excuse me for interrupting, but... How do you know that I like helping people?

—I just know.

—"Such a mysterious man, he must know me from somewhere, but I simply can't recognize him despite his peculiar sense of familiarity."

—This island is privileged. It is a peaceful island of peaceful people, and you are a beacon of light. You will come and go from it. It doesn't matter if you see the madness of the world and all the chaos that exists and will exist in it. In the face of adverse situations, you must remain strong and firm.

Although I interrupted him several times at the beginning of our conversation, I eventually went silent when I realized that the things he was saying were not common or mundane, but of vital importance to me and my future:

—We must continue raising the frequency of vibration.

—How do we raise our frequency?

—To raise the frequency, we must be one. A unity. That is the great deficiency today. There is a lack of unity.

After a brief silence in which I reflected on what he had already said, he began talking about the importance of children:

—Children are very important and delicate. They must be properly cared for, raised in a positive environment, free from toxic thoughts and contaminating habits. You must not judge based on the definitions of good or bad. There are no such things. The only thing that exists are different decisions chosen under different types of consciousness. If there is light and darkness, it is so you can learn to discern one from the other and make the best decision for yourself.

In a conversation like this, every word he spoke only increased my desire for the journey to not end yet, so I could continue hearing the celestial wisdom he was sharing with me.

As expected, at some point in time, we reached a roundabout, and the road to the right would lead me to the street that preceded what would be the end of my destination:

—At the roundabout, I'll take the right turn; I think I can drop you off here.

—That's fine.

—I'm not sure if your route continues in a different direction than mine. I think I'll park here.

—No problem, but remember what we talked about: don't change.

I remember very clearly that after hearing those words, I looked back to thank him for the pleasant conversation, as it was very unusual to meet people who spoke in such a particular way. But what was even stranger was his disappearance when I said goodbye.

I didn't hear the door open when someone exits, and I certainly didn't hear any words indicating his departure. I didn't hear the door close, nor any footsteps on the pavement. I checked the side mirrors and the rearview mirror in amazement, but I still couldn't see him. I repositioned my car carefully to ensure I wasn't in violation of any parking laws, and I searched within a 20 to 30-meter radius.

It was 2:30 PM, and people were supposed to be having lunch at the bar or restaurants, but that afternoon, there wasn't a soul on the street, except for two cars moving between the speculative silence of the surroundings and the stillness that mystery grants to those who face it. It was impossible for him to have left without making any movement. I knew that so much beauty and wisdom couldn't belong to this world.

My intuition and heart told me that this momentary passenger was probably an Angel, as only a being of such a high rank could express themselves in such a way and carry an aura so characteristic of what might be considered divine. These words were the most important thing I learned from him:

—Continue being the way you are. Despite the adversities of the world, remain authentic. Eliminate fear from your life, for it serves you no good and only consumes you. Take refuge in prudence. Being prudent is good; living in fear is not.

A GOLDEN ERA

Time was running against me; I had neglected my preparation for my singing hour in front of the diners who regularly attended one of the restaurants where I performed a list of songs I had preselected. I only did this activity on weekends, as on the other days I had to stick to my main work schedule. I prepared as quickly as I could and headed towards my friend Bea's house.

That night, she and her two daughters would accompany me all the way to the meeting point, where my friend and singer Rudy was also waiting for me. As a courtesy from the restaurant owner, every time I performed, I had dinner and drinks provided at the restaurant's expense. Interestingly, that night I wasn't hungry enough to enjoy the delicacies offered to us, so I limited myself to consuming liquids and non-alcoholic beverages. Personally, I don't like going out too late, especially late at night, because the road hides untold secrets, and occasionally, there is some unfortunate drunk driver disturbing the safety and integrity of other civilians. Once I showcased my dress while performing the songs on the small stage, I sat down to talk with Bea to let her know that I would be leaving for home earlier than planned. She understood and wouldn't be left alone, as her other friends were also present at the table.

On occasions when the journey was longer than the one we made that night, she would accompany me both ways, caring only about my well-being and safety, both on the street and on the road.

After saying goodbye to Bea and her daughters, Rudy, and other acquaintances who were going to watch me sing, I left through the main door and proceeded to start the car to make my route back. To avoid feeling so lonely in the darkness, I turned on some music on the radio. It was a quiet trip with no complications of any kind. It was around 11:15 PM when I was nearing my destination, and with less than 100 meters to go, I noticed in the field to my left what at first I thought would be an impromptu party with lights, holographic projectors, and multiple themed light sources. However, this assumption transformed into a strange and comforting paranormal sense of familiarity that would mark me for life. An intense, astonishing, and stimulating situation. Multiple ranges of sensations and different emotional ranges began to flow through every cell of my being.

My mind had ceased, and my attention had been amplified. Due to the extraordinary presence of what was manifested before me, I left the car in the middle of the road and got out of it in a state of disbelief and confusion at the sudden event that had occurred. I was three meters away from those faceless beings who emanated light in all directions while floating above the ground at a height of approximately six feet and five inches. I should mention that I wasn't alone, as fifteen meters to my left, there was a boy walking his dog along the edge of the field. The dog noticed the luminous presences and began to bark, eventually calming down and assuming a posture of a gentle and playful pet

Of course, the dog's owner also fixed his gaze on the light beings, but the disturbance to his psychological foundations caused by the anomaly he witnessed led to an unconscious flight response, taking the dog with him in the opposite direction of the visitors.

I felt no fear or dread about what might happen to me, as the sensations they transmitted and generated in me were of benevolence and peace, reaching the limit of happiness where laughter transforms into tears, in order to express the most profound feeling that seemed as though it would last for the rest of eternity.

When I directed my gaze upward, the three luminous bodies of light spun on themselves as if dancing in harmonic synchrony while rotating on their axis in a clockwise direction. From the most respectful position and attitude I could adopt toward them at that moment, I spoke timidly:

—Hello! Hello, and thank you for coming here.

In the face of something so dazzling, I could express nothing but my gratitude and happiness. I was almost hypnotized by their continuous clockwise rotations, which were as elegant as they were enchanting; a subtle essence could be felt in the air, along with a nearly imperceptible vibration. I made many attempts to communicate with them, but they did not look at me nor pay me any attention, as if they were ignoring me or had not sensed my presence.

I knew they would not stay long on Earth and that soon they would go to another place in the cosmos. Gradually, with their continuous rotations, they began to blur slowly until they completely vanished under my attentive and captivated gaze. When they left, I stayed for a few minutes, contemplating the desolate field, while reflecting on the mysteries of life and the universe.

How were they able to observe if they had no face or eyes? Why did they spin in such a strange and peculiar way? How do they travel through existence? Are they galactic beings? Hyper-dimensional beings? Spirits of the third heaven? I returned home, entered my room, and began to cry from the emotional shock of positivity.

They said nothing, refraining from any action except for their spins. My son and his father heard me cry incessantly until they decided to knock on my door and ask what was happening to me. I said to them:

> —I saw three beautiful beings in the field, made of a substance similar to a translucent, luminous, and energetic crystal-like material. They were very tall, probably over three meters high, and were floating above me...

Several days later, I encountered the guy who was present that night, but he reacted poorly to my question about what he had seen:

> —Don't talk to me, you're weird. Because of you, those things appear here. I saw how you went under them while I was leaving.

I didn't say anything to him; it wouldn't make sense to try to explain what had happened. There are still people who aren't prepared to understand experiences beyond what we encounter in our cultural daily lives, and when they come into contact with the strangeness of the unknown, they are possessed by an indomitable force characterized by an overwhelming fear that prevents them from going beyond the limits of their mind.

I stopped giving importance to the rude comment from the young man and continued with my day, which, curiously, changed when I was meditating and heard voices saying:

> —We are here, we have never abandoned you.

> —Who's speaking? Who is this?

> —We are here, we have never abandoned you.

I heard this phrase three times during my meditation, and I found myself forced to open and close my eyes to check where the voices were coming from. They sounded both inside and outside of me. The voices had a tone and quality that no human being could ever replicate, even with the best singing techniques available.

After returning from my deep meditative session, I went down the hallway to see if my son was around so I could share the experience with him and the new feeling I had. I found him just leaving his room, so I approached him to tell him:

—Alex, while meditating, I heard some very strange voices communicating with me.

—What do you mean, mom?

—I don't know, son, but I feel like I have some kind of powers. Let's go up to the terrace. Tell me, what would you like to see right now?

—Hmmm… I want to see white doves! Lots of white doves!

—You heard that, God, he wants to see white doves.

And just as we asked, a large flock of white doves appeared when we went up to the terrace:

—Wow, mom, you really have powers!— my son exclaimed at the impossible coincidence.

The next day, we had to meet with a private tutor who was in charge of giving Alexander his classes, so we had breakfast, got ready, and got in the car to leave. On the way to our meeting, we began talking about the sudden appearance from the night before:

—Mom, ask for the doves again.

—Listen to him, God, he wants doves, and I want them too.

And again, just as it happened before, a new flock of doves appeared, fluttering over our car before disappearing into the vast sky.

Other marvelous experiences that I began to live occurred when I was in charge of managing a beauty salon, of which I was the administrator, mainly because the owner didn't know anything about the beauty business. Although I only stayed three months working there, my desire was to change my life, break out of the routine, live new adventures, and travel to meet people, teach, and learn.

I didn't know what direction destiny would take to fulfill my request, but the paths that open up from time to time are mysterious. Just a few seconds after asking, I received an unexpected phone call from an unknown number.

I answered normally, and it turned out to be an acquaintance I hadn't heard from in a long time. We started talking, and he offered me an invitation to travel to Hungary for a week and meet his family. At first, I thought it would be crazy to take such a sudden trip, but then I remembered my request for a change in some aspect of my life. During my stay in that country, incredible things happened to me, phenomenal events that followed the same positive line as the rest of the occurrences.

In the family house in Hungary, there was a large expanse of wooded land that was very appealing to anyone who loves nature. Interestingly, the homeowners were always accompanied by their bodyguards, as they were a wealthy family of high social status.

So, when I decided to go to the forest to enjoy the pure oxygen from the trees, two bodyguards were assigned to accompany me for my protection and safety to avoid getting lost in the thick area. As I approached the trees, I felt an intense feeling of gratitude for their work, so I performed a small bow of respect, similar to the one Japanese people do, except my hands weren't at my sides; they were one on top of the other, placed on my chest while keeping my eyes closed. I held the bow for a few seconds before returning to my original position.

After making this gesture, I opened my eyes and was petrified by a new dimension of nature that I had never known before.

Was I dreaming? Maybe hallucinating? It would be impossible for people to believe me if I told them. I had forgotten that I was accompanied by the two bodyguards, who had followed me from a distance, so now there were three of us admiring the trees, which, in front of us, made a gesture that only happens in fantasy stories and adventure movies.

If we say that animals can communicate and express attitudes, we should now also know that beings from the Plant Kingdom have their own expressive abilities, which, hidden at times, emerge in unique and unrepeatable situations and conditions. A group bow from the trees I had just greeted? Now I know, along with those two armed companions, that such events are possible and real in the world.

We returned to the main house, feeling a pleasant sensation for having experienced something so special. In my case, I felt a strong urge to cry from the emotion and privilege of having experienced it firsthand. We got ready to meet the host to tell him about the event we had just witnessed in his forest, which he found very strange and didn't pay much attention to, as for him, it was impossible.

Days later, while still visiting the various neighborhoods and streets of Hungary, I asked God for the next thing I wanted to do, which was to give conferences. In less than seventy-two hours, I already had one organized for Hungary, and another one later in Vienna, all expenses paid. But it didn't stop there, as by chance, people began offering me all kinds of gifts, such as extremely expensive clothing, mink coats, and even an exclusive sheep-skin coat that I truly felt sorry for receiving. In this way, positive and pleasant days and weeks continued, ever since I interacted with those beings of light that floated in the air and spun around in beautiful sequences of movement. I always assumed they were angels, but perhaps they have a different name where they come from.

THE MAGICAL TAXI

It was a day in 2017 when I was preparing to attend a meeting that was scheduled that very afternoon, quite spontaneously, near a restaurant by the shore of a very well-known beach in the south of Tenerife. My friend Máximo was the one who invited me to this gathering and who would also be a guest of our friend Csaba, who was visiting the island at that time. However, I wasn't too keen on the idea of going to a house where I'd be alone with two men, so Máximo called his girlfriend Teresa to add another female presence to the plan. With this new suggestion, I agreed without hesitation and happily went after gathering everything I would need before leaving the house. When Csaba noticed my considerable delay, he came to see me personally, making it unnecessary for me to use my car to get there. The dinner went on without interruptions, with harmony and communal happiness prevailing as we enjoyed a delicious Russian salad and tasty potato croquettes, alongside a refreshing tropical soda since I wasn't consuming alcohol at that time, let alone animal meat. After a hearty and satisfying meal, I was ready to head back home to see my son, with the difference being that, on this occasion, I would have to wait for a vehicle that could take me to my destination. Although there were available cars, Csaba and Máximo were quite intoxicated from the carnival festivities of those days.

They insisted that I stay the night at Máximo's house, which had three rooms, and they made it clear that finding transport at that time of night would be extremely difficult.

I didn't give up and decided to call the taxi service, but their response was, to say the least, depressing, informing me that I would have to wait at least three hours for a car to become available, as most had traveled to the north of the island for the mass transportation of people, mainly festival tourists. I didn't mind waiting as long as necessary to travel, as I was firmly determined not to sleep at anyone's house. The seconds passed, and the wait became more discouraging with the thought that the chance of finding a car to take me seemed nonexistent.

I tried to stay as calm as possible, but I began to feel a little uneasy, just a little, until one of the most luxurious and exclusive taxis I had ever seen appeared. It was clear that it was an old and collectible model, likely produced in limited units, and with its light beige color, it exuded elegance and refinement. More mysterious than the sudden appearance of that beautiful four-wheeled machine was the curious and peculiar person who was driving the vehicle. With very small steps, an elderly man, with silver-colored hair indicative of his advanced age and experience, got out of the driver's seat. He was wearing an old shirt known in America as a "Chacabana," typically worn by older Cuban and Dominican men, with the shirt and pants both being white. His physical appearance resembled what my 100-year-old grandfather might look like, but with ten or fifteen more years on him. However, there was something about him that stood out immensely, like his barely perceptible wrinkles.

He approached us, searching for me:

—Carmen?

—Yes, it's me.

—Please, come up. I understand you're looking for a taxi.

Finally, I had a driver at my disposal, but one of the guys suggested that I dismiss him due to his elderly appearance.

—Carmen, don't get in this car with this man. He probably doesn't have the motor skills to take you home, it's better if you stay.

I didn't care what he said, as I had already gotten into the back seat even before he had finished speaking. With the seatbelt fastened and ready to go, the man started the car and accelerated. This is when the situation shifted from a pleasant vacation evening to a series of surreal events inside the taxi. As soon as I sat down in the passenger seat, I noticed the unmistakable scent of a type of flower with an incomparable fragrance. Then the driver got in, put on his seatbelt, and pressed the gas pedal. I saw him press it, but when I looked out the window, I realized we would never arrive, that we would never reach the destination. He seemed to notice that I had realized the anomaly, as he began to talk to me when he sensed my slight anxiety from the peculiarity of the situation:

—You know, my dear, in this transition we are going through, in this carousel that's spinning round and round, things are relatively fine, but when the events start happening all around the world, it's important to maintain peace, oh yes, very important. If man still doesn't understand what love is, there will be nothing left for him but to prepare for his destruction. There is still a chance for salvation, and it's through increasing the vibrational frequency of human consciousness. Love is forgiveness.

While I listened attentively to his words, I realized we were getting closer to my neighborhood, but when I looked outside again, I saw that we weren't moving:

—Excuse me, sir, but aren't you too old to be driving? I don't know if you've noticed, but it seems we're not moving forward.

—Age doesn't exist, my dear, it really doesn't exist. As for whether the car is moving or not, don't be like men who are always in a hurry and pressured to do things. One must live with harmony, peace, and calm.

After a few minutes, I saw that we had reached a crossroads, less than 30 meters away from the building where I would enter to get to my apartment. Before I got out of the car, the man said a few more words to me:

—You know, my dear, keep being who you are.

I thanked him for the compliment and prepared to pay for the almost endless ride. In my attempt to complete the payment for the service, the driver declined my money, saying that where he was going, it wouldn't be of much use to him, and that it was better if I saved it for some other expense. Puzzled by his peculiar behavior, I kept the ten-euro note in my wallet, thanked him once again for the ride and the conversation, and proceeded to get out of the car, carefully closing the door with the intention of not causing any damage to such an expensive vehicle.

Numerous and mystical are the experiences I've lived, but none like the one that happened after closing the door of that taxi, sent who knows by whom, maybe by God himself.

As soon as my hand left the door, a vehicle more than seven feet long would instantly disappear before my eyes. I blinked rapidly in astonishment at its sudden vanishing and looked in all directions, back, up, left, right, but found nothing and no one.

I ran as fast as I could to reach the building's door and quickly climbed the stairs to calm myself and reflect in my room on that extraordinary event. After entering the apartment, I saw that my son was about to go to sleep, but upon greeting me, he noticed my pale face, which alerted him that something wasn't right with me. After asking me what was going on, I told him honestly to ease his worry:

—A very, very old driver brought me from the beach in a luxurious taxi that seemed to be standing still. I reached the corner of the block, and as soon as I got out and closed the door, the driver and the car disappeared. I simply closed the door, and they weren't there anymore.

The identity of the driver who took me that night is something I will likely never know in my life. Where did that car go? I'll never know.

Despite the lack of explanations for the seemingly impossible events, I take the message I received that night from the kind driver and share it with everyone reading these lines:

>—There is still a chance for humanity to change, and it's through love.

BIOGRAPHY

My life has been a series of events in which I have navigated through an endless array of moments with different emotional tones. A sea of varied feelings and experiences from which I have learned, understood, and empathized with the suffering of others. These hard-learned lessons have enabled me to assist in healing the pain of others. After all, I came to this world with a mission: to heal. This mission continues, and I keep moving forward with it.

When I was seven months in my mother's womb, I was crying inside her. I know the reason for my tears: I didn't like the world I was about to witness. I was scared, thinking of all the things I would have to face. I wanted to live this experience, but theory is one thing, and practice is another. This life has been intense for me, filled with tough lessons that have taught me a great deal. I have lived through many beautiful and terrifying experiences, and I hold so much love within me to give to others. Thanks to this immense capacity for love, I realize that it is a great gift to love unconditionally, without knowing hatred. Since I was a child, I could sense when someone was about to pass away. When I told my family, they would become frightened because, a few days later, the person would indeed die. People couldn't understand why I said such things. On multiple occasions, one of my relatives accused me of being responsible for the person's death simply because I had said they would die, which burdened me with guilt and caused me severe headaches.

I hope that person didn't truly believe what they said, perhaps they were just afraid of such a bizarre situation.

I regularly continued to see the deceased until I was 41 years old; they appeared to me throughout my life. I coexisted with them, though it wasn't something I enjoyed or found amusing. I felt pity for their situation. Other times, I felt joy because they came to say goodbye in a more proper and tactful way. Some had emotional debts with their loved ones and gave me messages to deliver on their behalf. During much of my childhood, I experienced situations that were complex and difficult to explain to my family or anyone else. At night, the spirits of the deceased frequently visited my room, though I never felt fear toward them. I could see people who were no longer part of this life experience, though at the time, I didn't think of them as deceased, I simply saw them as beings and didn't question their presence.

Occasionally, there were special moments involving recently deceased loved ones whose spirits materialized at the foot of my bed. These events led me to an understanding I've had since childhood: the physical things we see and touch in this world are not all that exists. There is also what we call the Invisible World, the Ethereal Dimension, or the Spiritual Paradise. Faced with such extraordinary situations, I experienced an internal struggle throughout my life. Not understanding what was happening to me, I didn't accept myself, which made me ill.

Then came the year when I finally accepted myself and realized I needed to love myself just as I was. When I truly began to value myself, I freed myself from all harm, creating a clear before and after in my well-being. Going back to my childhood, while other children entertained themselves with games of the era, I found happiness in observing the sun, marveling at the majestic flight of dragonflies, or delighting in the beautiful flutters of butterflies in the vegetation during my long, solitary walks.

I remember those days when the rain fell to refresh and rejuvenate the earth, though everyone else complained about it. My appreciation for rain was entirely opposite; I cherished the drops of water the sky gifted us, so much so that I would go out into the patio to bathe in the rain, thanking it and merging with it.

There were times when other children found joy in harming lizards or other animals. I cried and tried to stop them because I knew they were doing harm to another being. While they played basketball, baseball, and other sports, I had the habit of laying a blanket on the ground and doing different positions and stretches that relieved my muscle tension—sometimes even on the wooden floors of my house. I didn't know exactly what I was doing since we had no access to books or magazines in those days. Later, I discovered that those stretches and positions were yoga. This made me happier, entertained me more, and made me feel much better.

At school, while other children drew pictures of their families, pets, or the typical house with the sun, my creative and artistic abilities went beyond what could be considered "normal" for a child my age. I stood out by drawing peculiar flowers with a distinctive fractal geometric structure.

These works puzzled and confused some teachers who couldn't understand what I was drawing. Over time, I discovered that these unique floral representations were mandalas.

In adolescence, while my friends were eager to attend parties in the villages, my attention and priorities were elsewhere—like taking cooking or sewing courses. I constantly sought learning, knowing it would bring something useful to my life. I was happy learning to sew, even though I was never particularly skilled at it. My joy in life resonated on a higher frequency, the frequency of love. The ultimate and first frequency, the one that has always existed and always will.

As a public figure, I was interviewed by various people, organizations, radio stations, television networks, and more. Although I was shy for more than a quarter of my life, I overcame that shyness at 27. Once I revealed my personality, nothing stopped me from sharing the wisdom I had acquired over the years.

This book has been prepared for those who seek answers to unresolved questions and are eager to know more today than yesterday.